Candice Brathwaite

CUTS BOTH WAYS

Quercus

QUERCUS CHILDREN'S BOOKS
First published in Great Britain in 2022 by Hodder & Stoughton

1 3 5 7 9 10 8 6 4 2

A CIP catalogue record for this book
is available from the British Library.

ISBN: 978 1 786 54183 3

Typeset in Adobe Caslon by Avon DataSet Ltd, Alcester, Warwickshire

Printed and bound in Great Britain by Clays Ltd, Elcograf S.p.A.

The paper and board used in this book
are made from wood from responsible sources.

Quercus Children's Books
An imprint of Hachette Children's Group
Part of Hodder & Stoughton
Carmelite House
50 Victoria Embankment
London EC4Y 0DZ

An Hachette UK Company
www.hachette.co.uk

www.hachettechildrens.co.uk

For 'Drumline'

Some would say it's better to be
judged by twelve than carried by six.
Always remember either way many
lives are changed forever.
Walk easy.
I love you.

Cx

CHAPTER ONE

My hand was trembling like it always did whenever I listened to it. But I pressed play anyway.

> *Yo, Cyn . . . Cyn . . . they got me, man – they came out of nowhere. I've called an ambulance, but I don't know . . . Cyn . . . it hurts, man. I want Mum. Cyn, get Mum.'*

I pressed my palms hard against my closed eyes, willing the tears to stop, reaching behind me to flush the toilet, even though I hadn't used it. Ever since Big Mike died, when I had to cry I would go to the bathroom. I'd cry as quietly as possible but sometimes the sobbing would grip me in the throat and a wail would escape. So I got used to keeping one hand on the flush. Finally, when I'd gotten control of my breathing again, I stood up and looked at myself in the mirror.

It was a different mirror to the one I'd cried in nearly every morning for the last two years. But it wasn't just the mirror that was different. Everything was. I shook my head to dislodge the memories. I'd only listened to that final voicemail from him so I could remember what his voice sounded like. I didn't want to remember the situation itself. I never did.

* * *

'Mum?!' I yelled, leaning over the banister. 'Mum! Do you know where my hairbrush is? Not the big one,' I continued, without waiting for her to respond. 'The small one, for my baby hairs.'

A moment later she appeared at the base of the stairs, all five feet of her. She was actually four foot eleven but insisted on rounding up. Her skin was as dark as mine but that's where the similarities ended. Mum was twice as beautiful. Even with a shaved head, there was a femininity about her that was undeniable. Among the unopened packing boxes, she moved gracefully.

'No, Cynthia, I don't. Have you perhaps tried the box labelled "hair things"?' she asked sarcastically.

Through gritted teeth, I sighed. 'Of course I have, Mum. Ugh, I'm going to be late,' I moaned, heading back to my bathroom.

My bathroom. I wasn't used to that yet.

'This wouldn't be necessary,' Mum said, ignoring the fact that I was already walking away, 'if you had just let your aunt braid your hair like I suggested. You knew this week was going to be chaotic.'

I chose not to answer, but as I closed the bathroom door she called after me, 'And last I checked, none of your hairs were ever wearing nappies.' I could hear her giggling at her own joke and I rolled my eyes.

I wouldn't have admitted it to her, but she was right. I should have just got my hair braided. But I didn't want *them* getting too used to *that*. We had only been in this area about five minutes and I'd already deduced that faces like mine were in the minus. When we first arrived, I'd kept my eyes peeled for a

2

Black haircare place but considering our nearest corner shop was over two miles away, I'd given up hope.

Now here I was, on the first day of my new school, with my hair looking like a cross between one of the Trolls and an electrocuted Barbie. Brilliant.

As I was pulling a wide-tooth comb through it, my phone began to ring. It was Jadell. Seeing her name immediately made me smile. We had been best friends since we were in reception.

'Gurl . . .' I sang, trying to put the phone to my ear and do my hair at the same time. If it were anyone else, I would have put the phone on loudspeaker but Jadell had a tendency to swear without warning and I didn't need my parents hearing that this morning. Mum wouldn't have cared but Dad would have hit the roof. He was mad conservative about things like that.

'Cyn! What's popping? You there yet?' she asked breathlessly.

'Babe, would I be answering my phone if I were? You know this is a fancy-pants-money-school. I can't just be whipping my phone out,' I reminded her.

'True, true,' she agreed. 'Listen, I'm just calling to tell you have a good first day and don't forget about us common folk.' She giggled.

That stung a bit. 'Don't start that nonsense again, I beg. You know I'm the same old Cyn,' I said, looking at myself in my bathroom mirror and forcing a smile, wanting to believe that.

'And you know what else is the same? The bloody number-two bus being packed as hell – Hold up – CAN YOU

3

LOT MOVE DOWN, PLEASE. SOME OF US HAVE PLACES TO BE! – Yeah, hello? Cyn, let me talk to you later, yeah? Good luck, babes!' she sang, and with that she was gone.

'Cynthia!' bellowed Dad from downstairs. 'You've got ten minutes!'

I sighed. I'd tried my best to wrestle my sprawling afro into something resembling a bun. Already it looked as if strands were trying to fight the green school-issued scrunchie. Ah well, it would have to do. One thing Dad wouldn't stand for was me being late on my first day. In his world reputation meant everything. I would need to hustle.

'So . . . are you excited?' Dad asked, his voice barely audible even above the very low car radio.

We had been in the car ten minutes before he decided to break the silence. This was awkward for us both, but I decided to indulge him.

'I guess.' I sighed, looking out at the endless fields of green that were whizzing past. The truth was I was petrified and annoyed. Petrified because I was being shot out of a cannon into a new atmosphere – two weeks into the autumn term, no less, when everyone else would have already settled in – and annoyed because I hadn't asked for this. If it were up to me, I would be on the noisy, packed number-two bus heading for Tulse Hill with Jadell. But instead I was in the middle of nowhere. OK, not *nowhere*, but Buckinghamshire wasn't exactly what I was used to. For starters, the school my parents had chosen for me was so far away and secluded I would either have to be driven or ride a special school coach to get there. I had gone from being independent and self-sufficient to basically needing a chaperone to leave the house. And even though I understood the reasoning behind my parents' interference, I couldn't help but think it was all grossly unfair.

'Now, remember, this isn't St Martin's,' Dad was saying. 'The teachers are going to expect more from you here. As am I,' he added. 'And don't forget that this is your GCSE year. You'll need to work extra hard and focus on your studies.'

'Yes, Dad,' I answered, because staying silent would have been seen as disrespectful.

'I'm sure your brother would have been expecting a lot from you too.' He sighed.

Would have.

Although it had been nearly two years, I still wasn't used to people speaking about my brother in the past tense. Though, to be honest, Dad had stopped talking about him pretty much as soon as he'd died. During the trial Dad had gone every day but would never tell me what was happening. Mum did most of the reporting back to me. It was like when Mike died, something in Dad had died too. Sure, he was always strict; his Nigerian upbringing would have it no other way. But he used to have a lightness, a swagger to him. Like how a president or a rapper walks into a room, *that* used to be my dad. Now he acted more like the secret service than the head of state, so serious, so quiet, it was hard to really see him at all. I let his suggestion sit there, prepared to be told off for staying silent. I even glanced over at him, trying to encourage it almost, draw

5

it out of him. But he said nothing. My bad mood deepened. And then, as if on cue, we began to wind up the tight country lane that led to my new school.

CHAPTER TWO

I knew which road led to my new school because I had been to meet Mrs Marshall, the headmistress, and hand in my registration forms the week before. That time we had taken a wrong turn and got lost, making me late by almost an hour. I'd prepared to offer up my pretend apologies, but the sturdy headmistress had actually apologised to *us* for the minimal signage that led towards the school. I had to keep my tongue pressed to the roof of my mouth to stop from laughing. It's funny how much people will overlook when you can pay the price.

Although I had already seen the school, the grandeur of it overwhelmed me again. Its dark-brown old brick, accentuated with even darker oak doors, made me think of medieval times. Usually approaching a place so clearly not built for someone like me would have led to some serious heart palpitations, but the three crystals gently knocking against one another in my blazer inside pocket helped calm me a little as I stepped out of the car. There was a rose quartz, a black obsidian and a citrine, all which used to belong to Mike. He was obsessed with anything to do with the ground – like actual dirt and rocks and stuff.

I remember when we were little he was captivated even with

regular garden stones and river rocks. Dad always had to force him to turn out the pockets of his school coat and trousers before coming home. 'Michael Adegoke, don't make your mother angry,' he would say, chuckling. 'If we have to call the plumber in yet again because one of your stones has jammed up the washing machine, I think she may look into giving you up for adoption.'

But as he got older, Mike became more serious about it. He'd spend ages online, looking through reference sites with diagrams of fossils, crystals and minerals.

I wasn't into rocks, but I'd envied Mike's ability to focus on something until he became an expert in it. I knew my dad was proud of that too. I'm more of a throw-it-all-at-the-wall type person. Which is *not* something Dad is proud of.

Weeks after Mike had been murdered, I finally plucked up the courage to go into his room. Standing there looking at everything laid out exactly the way he'd left it, I felt super overwhelmed. I know he was . . . *is* . . . my brother, but I admit I was scared. Haunted, almost. As I turned to leave, I spotted the rose quartz, black obsidian and citrine on one of the many shelves that held his crystal collection. They seemed to be apart from the others though. Not precisely arranged. Without a second thought I grabbed them, and I hadn't been without them since.

I tapped my blazer pocket, heard the satisfying *clink* and took a deep breath as we walked towards the headmistress, who was waiting for us at the entrance.

My dad and Mrs Marshall made small talk as she led us into the building. I looked around. The walls were decorated with plaques and old school pictures. There were trophy cases everywhere, which wasn't a complete surprise as when Mum was poring over the prospectus, she'd made a comment about how many sports were on offer.

'Look, Cynthia, they have everything – even hockey. I think you should give it a go. It would be good for you,' she'd said, not-so-subtly nudging Dad so he would back her up.

I'd smiled but not in a genuine way. We all knew that I had no interest in hockey. The only reason Mum had mentioned what sports were on offer was because of the weight I had recently gained – enough for her sister to make remarks about it. Even though I was closer to Mum than Dad, he and I were best friends when it came to the dislike of my auntie Jackie. Where my mother had seemingly been able to break away from toxic generational patterns, my aunt was stuck in the cycle – and permanently cross, or so it seemed. The only thing that gave her momentary joy was trying to press her sadness on to others. When she'd last seen me, she'd made it clear that she thought I would struggle to find a boyfriend if I continued to gain weight.

'And anyways, isn't grief supposed to turn you off your food?' she'd asked flatly.

Later that same evening I'd overheard Dad and Mum arguing. Dad was telling Mum that Auntie Jackie had spoken out of turn.

'When it comes to my children, dead or alive, I will not allow anyone to speak ill of them,' he'd said, and my heart had felt too small and too big all at the same time.

My mum had sighed so loudly I'd heard it from the stairs.

'You know Jackie struggles to mind her business . . . but Cynthia *has* gained weight since Michael . . . Maybe she needs to speak with a therapist after all.'

My dad began to protest, but I didn't get to hear the rest of the conversation as Jadell had called me and almost exposed my eavesdropping.

Now, pressing my nose against the monstrously sized trophy cabinets, I could see that Mum hadn't been exaggerating. Hockey, rugby, swimming and even badminton seemed to be popular.

'Do you play?' asked a husky voice.

I jumped and almost fell into the trophy cabinet.

'Whoa, you scared me!' I gasped, turning to face a very tall white boy. He was so tall that if it hadn't been for his uniform, I would have assumed he was a teacher. His dark-brown hair flopped to one side in an unruly manner and his eyes sparkled like two emeralds. I also couldn't help but notice that there seemed to be a cheeky glint in his gaze.

'Sorry. I didn't mean to,' he said, not breaking eye contact with me. 'I'm Thomas. Thomas Goddard,' he announced proudly, thrusting out his hand for a handshake.

Almost instinctively I rolled my hand into a fist and by the time I realised what I was doing, it was too late to pull back. But to my surprise he seamlessly closed his open hand into a fist, and we bumped knuckles.

'I'm Cynthia Ade—'

'Adegoke,' he finished smoothly.

I was impressed. It wasn't often that I met a white person who could pronounce my name properly *and* give a solid touch.

10

Perhaps it wouldn't be so bad here after all.

But meeting Thomas's outstretched hand with a fist must have irked my dad. I could feel him looking at me sharply, as if I had embarrassed him. Before I could apologise, this Thomas guy had stepped in between us.

'Hello, Mr Adegoke,' he said. 'My name is Thomas Goddard. I'm the head boy here at Thornton's. I'll be Cynthia's guide for today. And for however long she may need it,' he added, looking towards me with a grin.

Dad took Thomas's extended hand in his own and shook it vigorously. 'Very nice to make your acquaintance, Thomas. That's a solid handshake you have there.' He smiled. 'I trust that Cynthia will be safe in your company?' he questioned, his smile slowly melting away, still gripping Thomas's hand.

'Oh yes,' Mrs Marshall cut in. 'Thomas is a perfect representation of all that is good at Thornton's. Rugby captain, editor of the school newspaper and one of our best students. He and his brother certainly do the Goddard name proud.' She chuckled, making her large chest wobble to and fro.

I thought I saw a slight frown appear on Thomas's face, but by the time I'd blinked it had been replaced by a charming smile.

Dad finally let go of Thomas's hand. 'Right,' he said, in that way he does when he's done with something. 'Cynthia, I hope you enjoy your day. I'll be here promptly at four to pick you up. Mrs Marshall, Master Thomas.' He nodded at them both and then left me.

I cringed. *Master Thomas* – like, really? I sometimes wished that Dad understood he didn't have to prove himself to these people. I made a mental note to message Jadell about it later.

'Bye, Dad.' I sighed, turning my attention back to Thomas and Mrs Marshall.

'Right, Thomas, I will let you take it from here,' Mrs Marshall said, all in a hurry now that my dad had left. 'Cynthia, my door is always open. Well, unless it's lunchtime. I prefer to eat my tuna salad in peace!'

'Oh my,' Thomas said, half laughing as he watched Mrs Marshall practically run off.

'Oh my, indeed.' I giggled nervously. I couldn't have felt further outside my comfort zone in that moment. Fumbling around in my pocket, I let my fingers find one of Mike's crystals and I gave it a squeeze. *It's fine, Cyn. It's fine*, I repeated to myself. *You've got this.*

'Nervous?' Thomas questioned as he began to lead the way down one of the many hallways.

I didn't have the energy to front. 'A little.' I sighed. 'This place is just so . . . grand. It's a lot bigger than my old school.'

'Ah yes, I can imagine that St Martin's is very . . . different to Thornton's,' Thomas said.

I stopped abruptly.

'Fam, how do you know—'

He touched my elbow gently. 'Oh, don't be alarmed. I always research the new students that I have to take care of,' he said nonchalantly, as if running an Internet search on people was a respectable hobby.

My heart began to race. I wanted to ask him flat out *exactly* how much he knew about me. But I also didn't want to give him or anyone else cause for concern. Ever since Mike was murdered, I'd become aware that every move I made and every word I uttered was under a microscope.

'I really think we should get her a therapist,' I'd overheard Mum say to Dad one evening right before we moved.

She clearly hadn't let the idea go.

'Over my dead body,' Dad abruptly shot back. 'I already have a murdered son. I don't need the world thinking I have a crazy daughter too. The entire village back home will believe we are cursed. She will find her way. Life must go on,' he finished flatly.

I hadn't been surprised by Dad's words. His life had been so different to mine and Mike's. Born and raised in Nigeria. One of five siblings. Things were OK until his parents – my grandparents, who I'd never met – were killed in a car accident. Then Dad and his siblings went from attending private schools and fancy parties to being bounced around between family members who had all forgotten how well his parents had treated them when they were alive. As the eldest boy there was lot of pressure on Dad to make things better again. And he did his best. He left Nigeria and came to study medicine in the UK. He really grafted. Dad was harder on Mike than he was on me, and I always tried to remind my brother that it was only because Dad wanted the best for him. Dad was forcing him to study medicine even though Mike's heart was set on geology. But now Mike wasn't here. And I had to deal with the reality of Dad's coldness alone. It hurt. But I couldn't blame him. I wouldn't. Not like Big Mike used to.

With effort, I refocused on Thomas, who was still trying to defend his 'research' into me. 'Don't worry, I'm not an international super spy. I just like to be prepared. "Stay ready so you don't have to get ready," my brother always says. You'll meet him soon; he's in your form class. That's where I'm taking you now.'

I turned my attention back to the corridor. My old school halls had been bare apart from the occasional nursery-school-style display – scalloped-edge borders in bright colours, work held in place with Pritt Stick and staples. Here, though, every wall seemed carefully designed, covered in well-presented achievements, framed photos of classes, or packed trophy cabinets. As we walked, I tried to avoid making eye contact with passing students, all of whom were pretending not to stare.

'Right, here we are,' Thomas said, coming to an abrupt stop outside a grand door with a stained-glass window. 'Form 11C' read the wooden sign above the door. 'Your form tutor is Mrs Crabtree. She's a bit . . . eccentric.' He laughed, rapping his knuckles on the door twice and entering without waiting for anyone to respond.

Before I could question his very obvious lack of manners, he had ushered me into the room. Walking in was like crossing a threshold into another world.

It was so smoky that for a second I thought the room was on fire. But quickly my nose worked out the truth. It was the smell of Palo Santo incense. Mum burned it all the time at home when she was meditating. Once my eyes adjusted to the smoke, I could see that the lights weren't on and most of the students had their eyes closed. The few that didn't had now turned their attention towards me. I caught eyes with a Black boy in the front row. Even through my confusion over what was happening in the room, I had time to notice he was *very* cute. He had deep-brown skin, a similar shade to mine, but in the sort of smooth, velvety tone I wished my skin had, the kind that seemed almost immune to breakouts or acne of any kind. His jet-black hair was cut into a very sharp fade, with enough left on the top so his waves were perfectly pronounced. His eyelashes were as dark as the hair on his head, and their lushness gave his gaze a sleepiness that was almost hypnotising. I held his eyes for a few seconds longer before I felt an intense desire to look elsewhere. That's when I caught sight of Mrs Crabtree. Thomas hadn't been exaggerating when he'd said she was eccentric. She was wearing a brightly patterned floor-length dress and about seventeen different bangles on her arms, her hair in a bun way messier than mine on the top of her head.

Thomas coughed twice. I didn't know if it was to get Mrs Crabtree's attention or because the smoke from the incense was bothering him, but she turned towards the noise and when she spotted us, she walked over.

'Oh, Thomas,' she whispered. 'I forgot you were coming by this morning. Silly me. And hello, Cynthia,' she added, smiling at me. 'Let me just bring the class safely out of their meditation and I will be right with you.'

She faced the rest of the class. 'Now, 11C, we will soon be opening our eyes and coming back to a state of awareness. Before we do so I want you, as ever, to hold on to this feeling of peace. Should anything stressful or upsetting come your way today, remember how you felt in this moment.'

I felt Thomas nudge me in the side. When I looked up at

him, he was making a kill-me-now face. I tried to cover my snort with a cough.

'On the count of three, I'm going to ask you to open your eyes and return to the present moment,' Mrs Crabtree went on in her soft voice. 'One. Two. Three,' she whispered.

The students who hadn't already been staring at me followed her instructions. It took a few seconds for the atmosphere to readjust to something approaching a normal classroom. Mrs Crabtree turned on the light. 'Now, before I let you all go on to be your best selves, I would like to introduce our new student, Cynthia *Ah-day-go-kay*.' She beamed, clearly very pleased with herself at her pronunciation of my name.

I responded with a coy wave, which I instantly regretted. But it must have been enough as most of the class smiled and then went back to talking to each other and going through their bags. I was at once grateful and comforted by the soft hum of the classroom.

'Cynthia, I expect everyone will be more than willing to help you but if you need anything, my door is always metaphorically open,' Mrs Crabtree said. She turned to Thomas. 'Why don't you introduce Cynthia to your brother so she has someone with the same timetable as her to buddy up with?' she suggested, as the class began to file out of the room.

'Good idea, Mrs Crabtree.' He smiled tightly. 'Isaac, would you mind?' Thomas asked, turning to the front row where a tall white boy, who I guessed must be Isaac, was already standing up and walking towards us. Height really did run in that family. Next to Isaac, the cute Black boy I'd caught eyes with when we'd walked in was still staring at me as he

16

slung his rucksack over one shoulder. I couldn't help taking one moment to quickly look him up and down. I had just about got my head around the fact my family were the only Black people in the village. I had prepared to be one of one at school. Now I come to find not only is there another Black kid here, but it's a hella fine boy in my class. Shit, I needed to text Jadell ASAP.

I turned back to Thomas, realising I was being rude, and forced a smile on my face as the tall white boy reached us. But instead of stopping, the boy just gave me a nod and walked past us out of the door. Confused, I turned back to Thomas, just as a deep, smooth voice spoke out from behind him.

'And how can I help?'

'Cynthia, meet Isaac, my brother.' Thomas gestured.

'It's nice to . . .' I trailed off once I realised who Isaac was. It was the Black boy who had been staring at me since I came in the room.

He chuckled.

'You look like you've seen a ghost.'

My expression must have betrayed my desire to not look confused.

'I know, we don't look alike at all, do we?' he smiled, playfully punching Thomas in the upper arm.

'Of course not. I'm much better looking.' Thomas punched him back.

I shook my head, hoping it would help make sense of things.

'Yeah . . . cool.' I half-shrugged, trying to look unbothered. But really my brain was scattered. How on earth were *they* brothers?

'I'm sure Isaac can tell you all about it as he walks you to maths,' Thomas said, as if he were reading my mind.

'Um, I thought *you* were my guide?' I asked Thomas, hoping neither of them could detect the nervousness in my voice.

'Is there a problem with me?' Isaac asked, turning to face me. It was then that I noticed he had two matching dimples on his cheeks.

'Many of them,' Thomas butted in, before I could say anything.

Isaac kissed his teeth, which sent a feeling of familiarity shooting down my spine.

'I'm playing, bro,' said Thomas with a smile, and Isaac's face softened. 'Cynthia, because I'm head boy, I meet new students on their first day. But since I'm not in your form, I can't take you to all your classes. I promise that Isaac is the perfect deputy.' He was gesturing with his hands as he spoke, as if he were practising to be a politician. 'I shall, however, make myself available during the common periods of freedom whenever you might need me,' he finished, bowing towards me exaggeratedly.

'Boy, bye,' I said, laughing.

'Bye,' he responded. 'Have a good day, Mrs Crabtree,' he added more loudly, before leaving the classroom.

There were a few awkward moments of silence before I couldn't help but mention it. 'Do you really think he thought I meant "boy, bye" as in "goodbye"?' I asked, trying not to laugh.

Thankfully, Isaac didn't seem offended on his brother's behalf. 'Who knows?' he said with a smile.

'Ah, Miss *Ah-day-go-kay*!' Mrs Crabtree called from her

desk. I turned to face her. 'I haven't yet had a chance to gather all the things you need, including your planner. But I do have your freedom pass!' She chuckled to herself. 'Old fogey's joke there, sorry. So this pass –' she handed me a small white key card – 'gives you access to everything. Your locker, some classrooms and, of course, lunch! Please try not to lose it as it's an absolute faff for admin to sort.'

Now that she was closer, I realised she smelled like a perfume my mother used to wear. I remember because whenever she and Dad used to go out, I would race to her dressing table and try some on. The scent momentarily transported me to happier times.

'For now, I suggest you stick to Isaac as closely as possible as he has the same timetable as you,' Mrs Crabtree finished, bringing me back to the present.

No problem, I thought, trying not to smile. *No problem at all.* 'Sure,' I responded aloud.

'Great. Great. Namaste to both of you.'

'Errr, namaste, Mrs Crabtree,' Isaac said, leading me back into the hallway.

Once outside, we locked eyes and burst out laughing. A few students who were walking by stared.

'What the actual f—' I threw my hand over my mouth as I quickly remembered this wasn't St Martin's. If Isaac was shocked, he didn't show it.

'Welcome to Thornton's,' he offered, holding his arms aloft and spinning around.

A shrill bell pierced the atmosphere and rendered us both momentarily deaf for a few seconds.

'Damn, we get the point,' I muttered shaking my head back and forth.

'Don't worry, you'll get used to it,' Isaac offered, directing me to the left by placing a hand on my back. It felt as if he let his hand linger half a second longer than was necessary, but by the time my eyes met his, said hand was firmly in his blazer pocket.

'I hope so,' I sighed, trying to rid myself of the nerves in my stomach.

'Right, next up we have maths,' he advised, beginning to walk briskly down the corridor. 'There are usually ten minutes between lessons, an unspoken fifteen if you're the teacher's favourite – but maths is with Mr Jordan and his only favourite is detention, so never be late for his lessons.'

'Got it,' I shot back, momentarily distracted by a deep vibrating from my inside blazer pocket. I knew it was Jadell as I had set her alerts to be six short buzzes in quick succession. I only had a distinct vibrating pattern for one other person. And I knew for sure they would never contact me again.

Isaac eyed me suspiciously, then grinned. 'Although they say phones are banned, they know we live in a hyper-digital connected world, so they'll mostly turn a blind eye if you keep it on silent.'

'Safe.' I smiled. 'Um, where are the toilets?' I asked. I desperately wanted to see what Jadell had sent me and update her on the fact that I wasn't the only Black kid in school.

'Around the next corner. Just before Mr Jordan's classroom,' he said pointedly, looking down at his watch.

I nodded, but I was no longer listening. I was already crafting a quick text message to Jadell in my brain. I was also trying to make sense of the hallways, but they all seemed so similar.

'The classroom is right there.' Isaac had stopped outside a door marked 'Girls' but was pointing two doors down. 'Do you need me to wait here? Or do you think you can find your way?' He smiled.

I clicked my tongue. 'Boy, bye.' I waved as I hurried through the bathroom door.

I could hear his laugher echoing on the other side. I laughed too, because I knew that *he* knew exactly how I meant it.

CHAPTER THREE

I knew I didn't have much time before maths, so my phone was halfway outside my pocket by the time I'd slammed the toilet seat down and allowed it to take the full weight of me. My phone was on fire. There was a supportive message and an embarrassing meme from Mum. A firm reminder from Dad for me to put my best foot forward and ensure I was outside promptly at the end of the day. Even Auntie Jackie had sent a good-luck text. I bet Mum had made her do it. I scrolled to Jadell's name, reading the texts she'd sent.

> Gurl, what's happening!
> Holla @ me man.
> I want 2 know everything.
> Imagine, Keisha is pregnant.
> Do you think she will finish?
> NE ways – speakin of boys? Any nice 1s?

To be honest, the news about Keisha didn't surprise me, and while it was juicy gossip, I had more pressing things to discuss.

The sound of the toilet door opening made me pause. It sounded like two people had come in.

'Urgh, Isaac is so cute,' a girl's voice announced.

'Agreed! But can we talk about the new girl?' a second voice responded. I felt the shudder of someone slamming the door of the cubicle next to me.

'So much to discuss! Did you hear about her brother?' the first voice said from near the sinks.

I felt my legs turn to jelly, though, luckily, I was still sitting down.

'Yeah – but I mean, I'm not surprised. All you ever hear about is gangs killing each other in London. Dad always says they bring it on themselves,' the second girl added flatly.

'Mum won't even go to London at night any more,' the first girl agreed. 'And, oh my god, did you see her *hair*? What on earth is she going to do with that for swimming? She looks so unkempt.' I heard a giggle.

I felt my chest begin to get tight. How I wished Jadell was here. By now she would have shoved both their heads down a toilet bowl. I just wanted to cry, but I knew that wasn't an option. I quickly pressed send on the message to Jadell even though I hadn't finished it, stood up and coughed loudly. I wanted them to know that they weren't alone.

There were a few seconds of silence before I heard the stall door next to me rattle again.

Without hesitation, I unlocked my cubicle and walked out. Two white girls were standing at the sinks, looking horrified. I purposefully chose the sink that was situated right between them.

'Um . . . we didn't know you were—' began the first girl.

'Shut. Up.' I used the mirror in front of us to look both of them dead in the eyes. I was shocked by my own reaction. I never would have shown such anger at my previous school. But this felt different. Personal.

'OK,' said the second girl squeakily, not even bothering to dry her hands. 'Molly, let's go,' she commanded sheepishly.

'Yeah, Molly. GO,' I yelled, making her jump.

Molly quickly followed her friend out, leaving me with only my reflection for company.

I wrapped my hands around the edges of the sink and used it to steady myself. The anger was so overwhelming I felt as though I could have ripped the sink from the wall and thrown it through the ceiling. Looking down, I could see my hands were shaking.

First Thomas, now Molly and her stupid mate. How many other people knew?

I started to wash my hands and then caught sight of my hair in the mirror. The slick bun I had gone to the trouble of creating this morning had already fought its way out of the expensive uniform scrunchie. I looked like a pineapple. I tried not to cry.

24

Once more I patted my inside blazer pocket and felt the familiar clank of Big Mike's crystals.

'This is so fucked up,' I half whispered, half cried to no one in particular.

'What is?' An already familiar voice came from the doorway, making me jump.

'Isaac! What are you doing in here? This is the *girls'* toilet, you know,' I snapped, not giving him a moment to answer my question.

'You were taking too long to come out, so I wanted to make sure you hadn't run off or something.' He shrugged and slipped inside, seemingly unfazed that he was walking into the wrong bathroom. 'Hey, hold on,' he said, as he leaned up against the sink next to me. 'Are you crying?' he asked in a soft tone.

'No!' I lied, spinning around to the sink to quickly splash my face with water.

I felt a firm grip on my elbow and I allowed my eyes to meet his in the mirror.

'Cynthia . . . it's OK, you know? I get it,' he said gently.

I felt my body become taut.

'Get what, exactly?' I spat back.

'I get how it feels . . .' He trailed off, sighing. 'How it feels to be forced to leave friends behind and begin again in a new place where no one can mind their own bloody business,' he went on, stepping back and looking at the floor. 'Molly and her crew are a bunch of Karens with nothing better to do than gossip about people they don't know. Don't let them ruin your first day.'

I wanted to ask how much he'd heard, how much he really knew, but I felt the distinct sting behind my eyes that meant if

I opened my mouth I was going to cry. I tried to swallow my sadness but on the next blink my tear ducts betrayed me and drops rolled down my cheeks.

'Ah no, don't do that,' he hushed. It seemed as if he was going to step towards me but thought better of it and instead reached across to grab a paper towel from the dispenser. He handed the rough paper to me and I quickly used it to wipe the tears away. He touched my elbow again, this time squeezing it purposefully.

Away from the hazy fog of Mrs Crabtree's classroom, I could see he had a small cluster of moles under his right eye. The deep tone of his skin worked hard to hide them but in the bright bathroom light I could count four in a row, like a small constellation of stars. I wondered what they would feel like to touch.

The shrill sound of the bell going snapped me out of it.

'Shit, *now* we are late.'

'Oh no, my dad is going to kill me if I get detention,' I replied, hastily turning back to the mirror and trying to fix my bun.

'And Thomas is going to kill *me*! Come on, let's go,' Isaac ordered, heading towards the door and holding it open for me.

We jogged up the hallway, me trying to work out how I felt about everything that had just happened while praying that this teacher would show more mercy than Isaac had claimed he would.

But if the man now standing in front of the doorway was in fact our maths teacher, I could tell we were going to have no such luck. A balding white man towered above us both. Between his snarl and pointless comb-over he reminded me of Mr Burns from *The Simpsons*.

'Master Goddard,' he began, looking Isaac up and down as if he were something repulsive. 'And Miss Addy . . . Addy . . .' He trailed off and glared down at his clipboard, not bothering to mask how difficult he found it to pronounce my name. '. . . go-kay,' he finished with a sigh.

'Sir, I can explain,' Isaac began.

Mr Jordan lifted up the clipboard, silencing Isaac.

'Miss . . .' He paused again and clearly decided to give up on pronouncing my name entirely. 'Seeing as it's your first day I will let you off with a warning, but I expect this not to become a habit,' he huffed, swinging his clipboard back and forth. 'But Master Goddard, I expect more from you. Especially with your brother as head boy.'

Even though I wasn't touching him, I sensed Isaac's body go rigid. It reminded me that Mrs Marshall had also compared the two brothers when she'd introduced me to Thomas, and clearly Isaac liked it about as much as Thomas had. My heart gave a pang as I realised that no one at this school would ever compare me to Big Mike as they'd never know him. Mr Jordan was still talking at Isaac and I tried to refocus on the conversation.

'. . . and, of course, I do have to set an example that tardiness won't be allowed. That will be a thirty-minute detention after school today, Goddard.'

Before I realised what I was doing, I felt my lips purse as I sucked my teeth. I instinctively threw my hand across my face but Isaac had clearly noticed. What started as a snort grew to a slow, unmistakeable rumble in his chest and soon became a wild cackle, head thrown back, mouth wide open, eyes closed in fits of laughter.

Mr Jordan and I looked at him like he was mad.

I gently nudged Isaac in the ribs to try and bring him back to planet Earth.

'I'm sorry, I'm sorry,' he gasped between breaths, trying to control himself.

Mr Jordan looked scandalised. Clearly he had never seen Isaac act like this before. 'Very well. Detention will now be an hour and your new friend here can join you.' He gestured in my direction and turned to head back into the classroom.

This time I kissed my teeth on purpose.

'Excuse me, should I make it two hours?' he asked sharply, spinning back round.

Thank god Isaac stayed silent this time. I could only imagine the noise Dad was going to make when he found out I'd got detention on my first day.

'I thought not. Now, let's go inside and try to get on with what your parents . . . and guardians pay me to do.'

The first lesson at my new school had not got off to a good start and yet, as I briefly locked eyes with Isaac, who mouthed a clear 'sorry', I somehow found myself smiling.

CHAPTER FOUR

By the time the bell rang for lunch I was starving and had a pounding headache. A solid hour of algebra followed by another hour of history was bound to do that. But the headache was more than that. These first lessons had shown me how advanced the education was at Thornton's. At my old school I was near the top of every class but here things were going way over my head already, especially in maths, which had never been my strongest subject. Thankfully Mr Jordan hadn't decided to call on me yet but I knew it was only a matter of time before he did.

As the chatter of our classmates buzzed around me in the history classroom, I looked over at Isaac. He had yet to move from his desk because Molly, one of the horrible girls from the bathroom, had asked for his help with something. She kept purposefully flicking her long straight blonde hair over her shoulder as he explained something about the Franco-Prussian War. I let my hand move towards my head and find my own hair. Was it really 'unkempt'? I should have heeded Mum's advice and had it put in braids.

I audibly sighed, frustrated with how out of place I felt.

Slowly the class began to empty, but still Molly was taking Isaac's attention.

Feeling awkward just standing there waiting, I threw my school bag over my shoulder and left the room, deciding to try and find the way to the lunch hall myself. I remembered Thomas pointing it out this morning and I was pretty sure I knew the general direction. I would grab something to go and spend the rest of the hour in the toilet texting Jadell. *Hopefully no one will come in and do a shit*, I thought. I found the idea so darkly funny, I couldn't help but let a giggle escape me.

'Share the joke, Ms Adegoke?' A voice came from behind me in the hallway.

I jumped a little and turned to find Thomas smiling at me.

'Jeez, man, do you get a kick out of sneaking up on people?' I frowned, annoyed that yet again I had been caught off guard.

'Only when playing sports.' He chuckled, holding his hands up as if to prove he meant no harm.

'Whatever,' I shrugged, clicking my tongue. 'Seeing as you're here though, could you remind me how to get to the lunch hall? I am *famished*.'

'Of course, that's exactly the type of thing I'm here for. I wouldn't be a good guide if I didn't think about you— I mean, about how hungry you must be.' He blushed slightly.

I ignored his embarrassment.

'This way,' he said, leading me down the hall to the right. 'So how were your classes? How was Mr Jordan?' he asked, once we'd fallen into step together. 'As my form tutor, he's OK, but Isaac says he isn't great as a maths teacher.'

'I did feel like there was some kind of friction between them,' I said slowly. 'Mr Jordan was a little harsh, to be honest. I mean, he's given me detention on my first day.'

Just then a student knocked into me as they rushed down the hallway.

'Hey, "excuse me" is free!' I hollered, momentarily forgetting my surroundings.

The student glanced back at me with a slightly shocked look on their face, but upon seeing my expression clearly thought it was best not to respond.

I kissed my teeth.

'My brother does that when he's cheesed off too,' Thomas said with a frown.

'*Cheesed off*? Can you not just say pissed?' I asked, laughing.

Thomas blushed again, rubbing the back of his neck. 'Mum doesn't like swearing. She says "cheesed off" and I guess it's rubbed off on me.'

He looked embarrassed and I felt bad for making fun of him, so I quickly changed the subject. 'Anyways, detention on my first day! It was your brother's fault too!' Even though I was kidding, I regretted saying it the second I'd finished speaking and saw Thomas's expression. He had come to a complete stop and was pulling me aside so we wouldn't obstruct the now busy hallway.

'Listen, Cynthia, I love Isaac, but . . . be mindful of him. He can be quite . . . volatile,' he advised sternly.

What did *that* mean? My pulse quickened but I stayed quiet, not wanting to seem too eager for Thomas to tell me more. When I was younger, one of the reasons I would get into trouble was because I wasn't 'slow to speak', as Dad would often say.

'It's nothing serious,' he added quickly, perhaps seeing the concern on my face. 'Just a bad temper. Gets him into trouble at school more than our parents would like. I wouldn't want to see you end up in trouble too. Anyway, don't worry about detention – I'll fix it. If you give me your number I'll text you before last period and let you know it's been handled.' He reached into his blazer pocket for his phone.

'Really?' I asked, a bit in awe of how confident he seemed about getting a teacher to waive a detention. It was as if the sun literally shone out of his ass. But something about this also felt wrong. Isaac hadn't seemed like he had a temper. He'd been nothing but kind to me. Especially after the run-in with Molly and her sidekick in the toilets.

'Of course. Number?' Thomas asked confidently, holding his phone aloft, clearly unconcerned about a teacher catching him with it.

I called out my number, trying to be nonchalant.

'Brilliant. I'll text you now so you have my number too.' He smiled.

I felt my own phone vibrate gently.

As if it felt my desire to change subjects, my tummy rumbled loud enough for both of us to hear.

'Good thing the lunch hall is right here,' he said with a smile, opening the door for me. 'Let me go and find us a table.'

I shuffled inside and the grandeur of the lunch hall took my breath away. I looked around in awe. It smelled sweet and rich, and that, combined with the warm tone of the wood floor, reminded me of the maple syrup Mum would slather on our pancakes when Mike and I were kids. I hadn't had those pancakes in a while. She used to make them on all special occasions like birthdays and first days of school, but since Mike was murdered, she'd stopped. That wasn't the only thing that had changed. Losing Mike had unravelled her in a way that was almost scary to witness. The impulsive and headstrong Mum I'd known had been replaced by someone who seemed to always second-guess themselves and their decisions. A part of me thought Dad had seen this and used it to his advantage. Mum had such a good support system in London – we all did – but when Dad said we were moving, he did exactly that. He *said* it. There was no asking about what *we* thought or how *we* felt. The Mum I had always known would have kicked and screamed, but this version of her just listened to Dad's command and followed it. It was then that I realised I hadn't just lost Mike, but Mum too.

'Cynthia? Errr, hello?' It was Isaac, clicking his fingers in front of my face.

I came back to reality.

'Oh, hi,' I huffed, rolling my eyes. 'You remember me now, yeah?' I smiled, trying not to give away how much seeing him with Molly had irked me. We'd literally met this morning – he didn't owe me anything.

He grinned widely, clearly enjoying himself. I noticed how perfectly straight his teeth were.

'Aww, Cyn, don't be like that, man. I would never leave you hanging!' He laughed, playfully punching my upper arm.

'Don't worry, your brother made sure I found my way to food in the end.' I smiled and nodded at Thomas, who was now waving me over to a table.

'I bet he did,' Isaac said flatly.

'Speaking of which, he says he will get us out of detention,'

I mentioned, hoping it would change the mood.

'Yeah, he's good at getting me out of things,' Isaac said, but he was frowning now. 'Listen, I can't stay as I have piano practice and I don't want Thomas having to come to my rescue again.' He paused, seeming nervous all of a sudden. 'But look, here's my number,' he offered, holding out a piece of perfectly folded paper. 'Text me if you need anything.' He shrugged shyly.

As I took the paper from him our fingers briefly touched.

We both smiled.

'Sure, thanks. Have a good practice.' I paused. 'Also, it's Cynthia,' I added.

'Huh?' he shot back, clearly confused.

'Earlier you called me Cyn. It's Cynthia. There are only three people who are allowed to call me that. My mum, my bestie and . . . my brother.'

'Ah, right. Gotcha. Bye, Cynthia.' I watched as he began to weave his way through the now heaving lunch hall.

'So what was that all about?' Thomas asked, once I'd reached the table he'd found.

I screwed up my face a little. 'Oh, nothing. He just gave me his number.' I held the small piece of paper aloft and shrugged as if it were nothing. But both the butterflies in my stomach and Thomas's expression said otherwise.

He quickly smiled. 'Well, now you have both our numbers. You can't go wrong with that.'

'I hope not,' I laughed, taking my blazer off and swinging it over the back of one of the chairs to claim it.

'Wait, it will be safe here while we get food, right? My

blazer?' I asked, not wanting to suffer the noise if I lost yet another one. At St Martin's it wasn't until I'd been three blazers deep that I realised I wasn't being careless, they were just being stolen by girls whose families couldn't afford to replace theirs.

'Um, yeah, it's not a Bugatti,' Thomas laughed.

His response reminded me just how out of my comfort zone I was. Of course no one was going to steal a *blazer* here. *Get it together, Cynthia*, I told myself sternly.

'Right, let me point out what's edible and what you should avoid,' Thomas began. 'Over there is the salad bar. That's usually OK – seven out of ten on a good day. The hot station can be hit and miss but it's great on Wednesdays and Fridays.'

'What's on Wednesdays and Fridays?' I asked.

'Wednesdays are Caribbean day and Fridays are fish and chips. Get here early! People will come back for seconds with no regard for how empty another's tummy is.' He chuckled.

'Caribbean day? Really?' I screwed up my face apprehensively. Since I arrived, I'd only seen three Black faces. One was Isaac's, the second was a window cleaner who happened to interrupt our maths lesson and was abruptly shooed away by Mr Jordan, and the third was my own, reflected in the bathroom mirror. I didn't want to be judgemental but what on *earth* would they know about Caribbean food?

'Don't make that face! The jerk chicken is slamming,' Thomas said.

I couldn't help but crease up.

'Slamming? OK, calm down, Jamal. I'll be the judge of that.'

'Erm, Jama—' Thomas began.

35

'It's a figure of speech. Don't worry yourself too tough. Oh sh— I mean sugar, I forgot my pass in my blazer.'

'Don't worry, I'm already on it,' said Thomas, heading back to our table.

As he hurried away, I suddenly remembered Mike's crystals. I hoped he didn't find them. I wasn't in the mood to talk about them now and I knew I wouldn't be able to lie. I raised to my tiptoes, but I couldn't see our table from my place in the queue. A moment later, he was back.

'Here you go,' he said, waving my pass in the air playfully.

'Thanks,' I said, waiting for the questions about the crystals to come.

'Your phone was blowing up,' he added casually. 'Must be your boyfriend.'

I scoffed and shuffled forward as the line began to move. 'Don't be silly. I think it's just my best friend.'

'So no boyfriend then?' he pressed.

'No,' I answered a little sharply.

'Got it,' he said, holding his arms up as if he were in a stick-up. 'I wonder if there are any croutons left,' he mused, changing the subject.

I looked up at him – I had to, he was so tall – and saw that he was smiling.

Once we had collected our salads and returned to the table, the first thing I did was check my phone. Almost all the messages were from Jadell.

GRL IT'S BEEN OVA 3 HOURS.

> **IS THIS A *GET OUT* SITUATION?**
> **SEND A TEACUP EMOJI IF U NEED HELP**

I tapped out a quick reply.

> **LOL ALL GOOD NO NEED 2 SEND FEDS**
> **I WILL CALL U 2NITE**

Just before I went to put my phone away, I spotted Dad had texted me too.

> Cynthia
> I trust that your first day is going well and you
> are positively upholding the Adegoke name.
> I will be waiting for you promptly at 4 p.m.
> Thank you

I rolled my eyes. He was forever concerned with the 'Adegoke name' and what people thought of us.

Well, me specifically.

He would never admit it, but I knew deep down, beneath the grief he carried for Mike, there was also shame. Back in London we couldn't escape the whispers.

All too often when young Black boys are stabbed to death, everyone silently decides that they must've been up to no good, that they – in this case, Mike – had it coming. It would take me becoming the first Black female prime minister for the Adegoke name to be cleared. And he knew it.

'Earth to Cynthia; come in, Cynthia,' Thomas sang, waving a hand in front of me.

'Sup?' I sighed, quickly stuffing some croutons into my mouth.

'Everything OK?' he pressed. He was watching me closely, looking genuinely concerned.

'All good,' I lied, pulling a taut smile over my face. 'So, do you know what my teachers this afternoon are like?'

He pulled a folded piece of paper from his blazer pocket.

'I hope you don't mind but I took the liberty of asking for a copy of your timetable from Mrs Crabtree. Just so I know where to meet you, of course,' he added quickly. 'So it's double English with Mr Sittenfeld, who's well liked, and then art is the last lesson of the day, which is back with Mrs Crabtree. Once we're done here, I'll walk you to English class, if you'd like?' he propositioned, raising an eyebrow.

'You know that's an offer I can't refuse,' I responded, suddenly distracted by how green his eyes were.

'Great,' he smiled, his lips turning up into a slight smirk.

The rest of the day passed in a blur. I felt less intimidated by what was being taught in English than I had in maths and found it relatively easy to keep up.

Mr Sittenfeld had seated me next to Morwenna, a red-headed girl who seemed shy and brainy. Though in my head I could hear Jadell calling her a top neek, she seemed nice, but I was thankful when she didn't try to make conversation beyond 'hello'. I wasn't here to make friends – I already had

38

those back home. Even though J and my crew were far away, they were still my girls and I wasn't about to let this posh school go to my head.

Once English was over, I followed the class back to our form room for our art lesson as Thomas had advised. When I reached it and saw Isaac already in his seat, I couldn't stop a smile spreading over my face.

He gave me a small wave as I walked in.

I let the other students bustle past me so I could assess which seat I might be able to park my bum on. The one next to Isaac was empty . . . Did I dare go over? Or were there assigned seats in this class?

'Oh, Cynthia!' Mrs Crabtree sang loudly, noticing me hovering awkwardly. 'Stephen has gone home early so feel free to occupy the desk next to Isaac for this lesson and I'll assign you a permanent desk first thing tomorrow.' She turned her attention to another student who was waiting nearby, 'Now, Julia, bear with me a second and I'll get your workbook.'

I shrugged my backpack off and dumped it on the desk with a bang, sliding into the empty seat next to Isaac.

'Rah, what do you have in there, boulders?' Isaac laughed, nodding at my backpack.

Sitting this close to him, my gaze was drawn to his lashes again. They were so long, he could make mascara jealous. His skin was smooth and flawless, even inches away. His shape-up was sharp and his black hair created deep waves, like Big Mike's used to. The thought of Mike quickly pulled me back down to earth and I looked away.

'Wow, you've got jokes, huh?' I scoffed, shoving my bag under the table.

'I'm just messing. How has your first day been?' he asked, turning his chair slightly so he was facing me.

'Well, if we overlook the toilet situation and the almost-detention, pretty well, considering,' I said lightly, before becoming serious. 'I honestly thought I was going to be one of one, so I can't lie, when I saw you it was a relief.'

He reached out and took my hand, placing it between his like a parent might to a sick child. 'I'm glad I could provide such comfort,' he said, mock serious.

I quickly snatched my hand away before he could feel my racing pulse. There was no mistaking the butterflies in my stomach. I shot him a sideways glance. 'So, uh, how did you get here anyway?' I pressed, desperately wanting to put the pieces of the puzzle together.

'*Uh*, by bus,' he said dryly, but quickly added, 'I'm messing, I know what you mean . . . but it's a long story.'

'I'm at this school for at least another year. I've got time.' I smiled encouragingly.

Before he could continue, Mrs Crabtree clapped her hands together loudly. 'Class, can I have your attention to the front, please?' she bellowed.

'Maybe another time,' he whispered, but he had the look of someone who had been saved by the bell.

CHAPTER FIVE

That evening I was curled up on a sofa in our conservatory, looking out into the darkness. Back in London, we didn't have nights like this. There were always lights – streetlights, car headlights, shops open late – and everything was so busy that you could hear the bustle of the city no matter what time it was.

It was different here. Some people probably thought it was peaceful. To me it felt eerie. Like the world had ended and no one had told me yet.

An endless black.

The memory came back in a rush.

We met with a woman who introduced herself as the pathologist in the mortuary, me clinging to Mum's arm. Dad was at a conference in Germany. Mum had been called in to formally identify the body. I couldn't let her do that alone.

When the pathologist introduced herself there was a sad finality in her tone that I refused to accept.

It might not be him, *I thought.* There could have been a mistake.

OK, his phone was going straight to voicemail and all of the texts I sent were marked as delivered but unread – but that wasn't proof.

Mike taught me to always look for proof. Evidence. Something real. Like fossils.

'If you know what to look for, they can tell you everything you want to know,' he would say, poring over images of rocks on his computer.

The room we entered was desolate aside from a rectangular table that held a person-shaped form beneath a stiff blue sheet. It was freezing, like someone had sucked all the warmth out of the room before we'd stepped in.

The journey from the door to the table took for ever and I was torn between rushing over and ripping the ugly blue sheet from the table and turning around right then and running out of the room.

I did neither. Instead I tightened my grip on Mum's arm, feeling her stiffen. A few feet shy of the table, we stopped, unable to go any further.

The pathologist approached the table and began to peel back the sheet. I felt like I was watching a film in slow motion, or that I was underwater. Every moment seemed to take an eternity.

Whoever this was, they had hair similar to Mike's. The shape-up was sharp and the waves came forward, swirling at the crown. Over the left eyebrow was a terrific bruise, loud and pronounced even on this person's dark skin.

As the sheet continued its descent, my heart began to pick up speed. His nose . . . it was so similar to Mike's. There was more bruising.

The lips. They were swollen and lopsided.

And then . . . the chin.

I felt my legs give way when I spotted it.

The Adegoke trademark. Dad had it, I had it and . . . Mike had it. A deep dimple buried in our chins.

That was unmistakeable.

'No. No. No!' Mum cried out, falling to her knees. 'My soooooooonnnnnnnnn!'

And then everything went black.

My phone vibrated, snapping me out of my thoughts, my memories of the worst day of my life. Jadell was calling. As much as I wanted to answer, Dad had made it clear that even the thought of relaxing was not an option until my homework was done.

I sent Jadell a quick text.

> Girl give me a few hours yeah?
> This skool h/w don't play!

This algebra homework was doing my head in. I had been sitting here for almost an hour and still couldn't wrap my head around it. If only there was someone who could.

'Isaac!' I said aloud.

Damn, there went my mouth moving faster than my mind again.

'Who's Isaac?' I heard Mum question from the doorway.

I startled. 'Er, just a guy in my maths class.'

'*Just* a guy?' Mum questioned, with a sparkle in her eye.

'Yep, that's all,' I insisted. It had been ages since she'd teased me like this and it dislodged the memories from that night that were still lingering in my head, making my heart feel a little lighter. But I wasn't ready to share the possibility of Isaac with her yet.

'I should hope so.' The bass in Dad's voice bounced off the glass and made me jump a little. I hadn't known he was within earshot. 'I'm not spending five thousand a term for you to play footsie under the table, Cynthia.'

'Yes, sir,' I responded mechanically, refraining from rolling my eyes. 'No need to worry about me, Dad. I'm not interested in boys right now,' I added, hoping to throw some water on this unnecessary fire.

'Is it girls you're into then?' Mum asked, failing to hide her amusement.

'V! That will be enough!' Dad choked, clearly horrified at the idea.

'What? It's not how it was for us back then, Baba.'

As embarrassing as this conversation was, it felt nice to watch them banter. I couldn't remember when I'd last heard them talk about something other than life admin or Mike. Maybe moving here had been what we needed.

But Dad's expression was souring. 'That's exactly the problem,' he huffed. 'Everything was better back then.' There was a sadness in his voice that indicated it wasn't just his childhood experiences he was talking about.

Mum reached for his shoulder but Dad quickly moved away, clearing his throat.

Out of the corner of my eye, I saw Mum stiffen and the atmosphere went cold.

'I'll be in my study until dinner is ready,' Dad said to no one in particular, before turning to me. 'Cynthia, focus on your homework, please. Remember that your GCSEs are mere months away.'

I saw Mum's shoulders drop and quickly looked down at my homework so she wouldn't clock that I'd noticed.

Staring at my maths, I was once again reminded of Isaac. I shot up from my chair and headed quickly to the stairs.

'Don't run!' Mum yelled after me.

I mouthed the second half along with her – *Cos I'm not going to the hospital today* – rolling my eyes.

Once in my room, I went straight to my wardrobe where my blazer was hanging. Searching through its inside pocket, I found my key card but nothing else. I checked the other pockets in case I was misremembering, but they were also empty.

'Where is it?' I hissed to myself. I'd definitely put the little piece of paper in my blazer pocket. Where could it—

Suddenly, I remembered another person who'd had access to my blazer today. Thomas.

'Nah,' I said aloud, full of disbelief.

I put the blazer back on its hanger and assured myself that I must have just misplaced it. But something in me – that feeling in my tummy that Big Mike had taught me was 'intuition' – wasn't entirely convinced.

'Did you see that, Cyn!? The lion has sick intuition; it knew that there was a threat nearby without having to see it,' Mike said, practically bouncing with excitement.

We'd been in the living room watching a documentary about wildlife. I must have been ten or eleven. Personally I would have preferred to watch cartoons or The Fresh Prince of Bel-Air *or something, but Mike had beaten me to the remote that day.*

'What's intuition?' I questioned, not taking my eyes off the TV.

'It's like an invisible machine in your body that sends you signals. Usually letting you know that something isn't quite right, or that you should leave a situation because you just know something isn't going to go well,' he'd explained, looking thoughtful. 'No matter what, always follow your intuition, Cyn.'

'How much longer of this jungle show, bro?' I groaned, only half paying attention.

It's funny the things that stick with you after someone is gone.

And right now, that thing – the feeling – Big Mike told me to look out for was screaming at me that I didn't just 'misplace' that piece of paper.

But why would Thomas get rid of Isaac's number? It didn't make sense. I thought back to Thomas's warning that I should steer clear of Isaac if I wanted to do well at Thornton's.

As if right on cue, Jadell's name flashed on my phone. I glanced at the clock, confirming I still had at least half an hour before Mum called me down for dinner.

I answered the call, closing the door so Mum and Dad wouldn't sneak up on me like they had in the conservatory.

'You'll never believe the day I had, J,' I said, sighing.

'Sis, tell me *everything*!'

CHAPTER SIX

'Yo, sleepyhead,' a voice cooed above me.

'Go away,' I moaned, turning my head in the opposite direction but the person moved so they were standing in front of me again.

'I would, but this isn't your bedroom, Cynthia.' It was a warm, amused voice.

Isaac!? Startled, I sat bolt upright, almost giving myself whiplash.

'Shit!' I hissed, remembering where I was. Thankfully, the room was still relatively empty. I'd been the first one here and the silence must've lulled me to sleep.

Isaac was laughing as he pulled out the chair next to me.

'Bad night?' he asked, eyebrow raised.

'Something like that.'

Aside from a rushed dinner in between our calls, I had spent most of the evening on the phone to Jadell, talking to her long past the time I should have been asleep. I had told her all about my first day, including all I could decipher about Thomas and Isaac. *Especially* Isaac.

'We could finally double-date!' she sang.

Jadell was 'dating' a light-skinned boy called Pedro who went to the local PRU – the Pupil Referral Unit, where students who were excluded from school were often sent – and travelled on a stolen moped. He was cute, but Pedro – much like his stolen bike – was someone else's property. He was a straight-up player and, worse still, everyone either wanted him or had already had him.

Not me though. Anyway, being dark-skinned meant I automatically wasn't his type. Like most boys my age, Pedro was only interested in the girls who were mixed race, racially ambiguous or light-skinned enough to pass as one of the former. Having been friends with Jadell since we were barely potty-trained, I had long ago become accustomed to the fact that her light skin gave her a pretty privilege that I would never have. Jadell never acted like she was better than me though. Beyond the fact that we were best friends, both her siblings were the same complexion as me, so she got it – that it was just a roll of the dice, a genetic lottery game.

So when I told her about Thomas and Isaac, two boys seemingly *both* interested in me, she was genuinely excited. And I found that I was too. I'd fallen asleep with a smile on my face.

Until Mum and Dad's arguing woke me yet again.

I'd hoped moving would have given us all a fresh start. But it was becoming clear that they had packed their issues along with the furniture. By the time I drifted off, it was 3 a.m. It felt like a minute later when my alarm went off at six. I'd set it early so I would have enough time to wrestle with my hair and get to school before first period – and because I hadn't yet finished the algebra homework.

When I arrived – Dad dropping me off with more instructions to 'uphold the Adegoke name' – I was so early the caretaker, who I later learned was called Mr Fitzgerald, had to let me into the library.

'You must mean business,' he chuckled, using one hand to toy with the lock and the other to balance what looked to be a piping-hot coffee.

When he finally opened the doors, the first thing to hit me was an old, oaky scent. The library I used to visit back in London was really just a room with a few books. This was clearly custom-made, with wooden shelves built into the walls, an upper level containing even more books, and squashy leather chairs tucked away in alcoves. It was like something out of *Beauty and the Beast*.

'It's magnificent, isn't it?' Mr Fitzgerald sighed. Clearly my expression had given it all away.

'It was losing its way a bit but then the Goddards made that wonderful donation . . .'

That name immediately penetrated my wonder.

'The Goddards? As in Thomas Goddard, the student?' I tried to keep my voice nice and light.

'Bingo! Yes, he comes from a long line of generosity, that one.' He tapped a plaque next to us, which did indeed honour the fact that the Goddard family had made a healthy donation.

I let out a soft whistle.

He left me with questions I was sure none of the books around me could answer.

And then, somewhere in between taking a picture of the plaque to send to Jadell and trying to get my head around Mr Jordan's homework, I must have nodded off.

'Yo, is this what put you to sleep?' Isaac was asking me,

gesturing at the open maths books in front of me on the table.

'Yep.' I smiled, hyper-aware of my appearance, quickly wiping my mouth in case I had dribble on my face.

'Man, looks like you need help. Why didn't you just call me?' he asked, pulling out the chair next to me.

I felt my heart rate elevate.

'Well, I thought about that but . . .' I trailed off quickly. My mouth was moving faster than my thoughts again. I'd nearly mentioned my suspicions about Thomas taking Isaac's note from my blazer pocket.

He raised his eyebrows, reaching for my notebook.

'But I misplaced your number,' I finished, not making eye contact with him.

'OK, let's solve that issue first. Pass me your phone,' he commanded.

If he was anyone else, I would have pointed out their lack of manners, but his sincere and determined tone made me melt a little bit.

I pushed my phone towards him. While he tapped his number in, I allowed myself to look at him, I mean *really* look at him. And to be honest he looked even better than I'd remembered. His skin was glowing and the waves in his hair were artfully brushed forward. He was close enough that I could make out the unmistakeable warm scent of cocoa butter and something sweet and woody. It reminded me of one of the many fancy colognes my father owned. Although I hadn't clocked it the day before, in this light the rumblings of facial hair were definitely present. Even though St Martin's was an all-girls school, I had been around enough male cousins and family friends to know first-hand that boys my age were usually immature. But Isaac was different. He appeared to be very grown up; *an old soul*, Mum might have said. Almost as if he had lived many lives before this one.

'There. Now, tomorrow if you say you've lost your phone, I'll know that you actually just don't want to talk to me.' He laughed, sliding the phone back towards me.

As I reached out for it, his hand touched mine. I froze, fighting against the reflex that wanted me to pull away. And so did he. For about five seconds we kept our hands still, just touching. Then my phone began to vibrate and we jolted apart. It was Dad. Unwillingly I grabbed the phone, cancelled the call and placed it in my blazer pocket.

'Not in the mood, huh?' Isaac asked without lifting his eyes from my notebook.

'Not at all,' I admitted flatly. 'Don't you just hate it when they act like you're still a baby, like you don't know what's going on?' I rattled on mindlessly, not knowing what I was saying, my heart still racing, the feeling of his warm fingers still imprinted on my hand.

'Who?' he asked.

'Parents! My dad, mainly. He just really does my head in, you know?' I moaned.

'Nah, not really. My dad died of pancreatic cancer when I was two. And then I lost my mum soon after that.' He said it matter-of-factly.

Shit, I thought to myself.

Shit. Shit. Shit.

Honestly, I had never wanted there to be a major earthquake

51

so bad. A small tsunami would do, actually. Heck, just the fire alarm would be great.

Now the only sound was the soft scratch of the pencil on my notebook as Isaac continued to try and make sense of my jumbled equations.

'I'm sorry,' I whispered, even though I knew first-hand that was never enough.

'Don't worry,' he offered gently, without taking his eyes off my notebook. I squirmed in my seat. 'I honestly can't remember them,' he went on. 'I think that makes it easier in a way. There's no sense of loss because I can't recall what it was like when they were around. I guess it's harder for people who . . .' He trailed off. Now it was his turn to squirm.

I knew it was now or never. 'I can't put it into words,' I began, a little afraid of my own voice. 'I still can't understand the fact that no matter where I go on this planet, I will never, ever find my brother again.' I exhaled.

'Do you miss him? Sorry, that's a stupid question,' Isaac added quickly, now turning to face me.

'Every day, every minute, every hour,' I whispered. It wasn't until a drop of liquid hit the table that I realised I was crying.

I went to wipe my eyes, but Isaac's hand got there first. Using his thumb, he gently swiped the tear away.

I felt my stomach do somersaults and, very briefly, I leaned my cheek into his palm.

'I get it.' He sighed abruptly, pulling his hand away and turning back to my notebook.

No, you don't, I said to myself.

'I get it,' he insisted, as if he'd heard my innermost thoughts. 'I have a brother too . . . a real one, not adopted. His name is Israel . . .' He trailed off, looking as though he was annoyed with himself.

I held my breath. I wanted to pry but I had already learned that pushing Isaac would only make him clam up. So we both allowed his statement to sit there and linger between us, like a heavy rain cloud threatening to burst at any moment.

'Isaac!' a shrill voice called.

We both turned to see Molly. *Stupid Girl Number Two*, as Jadell had christened her after I'd explained the showdown in the bathroom.

'Hey, Molly,' Isaac offered flatly.

'Hi,' she offered, looking sheepishly in my direction.

I raised my eyebrows in response and pretended to busy myself with my phone, spotting a text message from Dad as I unlocked it.

I trust all is well.
Please inform your mother that I will be in surgery until late tonight.

'I thought you were going to meet me before first period to review the homework,' Molly was saying to Isaac. 'We were going to look at those quadratic equations together.'

'Ah yeah, damn, sorry about that.' His tone didn't quite match what he was saying. 'I got carried away.' I could feel him look towards me as he said that.

'I can see that.' She giggled, clearly trying desperately to ease the ever-growing tension. 'I can't wait for your family's party on Saturday,' she added. It came out of nowhere and I could tell she was mentioning it to make me feel excluded. I continued fiddling with my phone, trying not to let her have the satisfaction of seeing my interest.

'Yeah, it's not really my thing, but you know the Goddards, they love tradition.' Isaac rolled his eyes, then nudged my foot under the table. I looked up. 'Cynthia, you up for a boring party?' he asked. 'It's this thing my parents put on for all the Thornton families every year. It's this Saturday though, so I understand if you and your family are already busy.'

'I'd love to come.' I smiled, praying I was showing more teeth than gum. I wasn't just saying I wanted to go because Molly was hovering like a hawk going in for the kill. Sure, that was *some* of it. But the shot of adrenalin I'd felt when his foot had nudged mine under the table was a much bigger part. Whether Dad would actually let me attend was another conversation entirely.

'Cool. Hit me up so I have your number and I'll text you back with the info.' Isaac was still staring straight at me. I had to stop myself from laughing out loud at the expression of dismay on Molly's face. Clearly this hadn't gone her way.

'See you in maths, Isaac,' she said shortly, turning away to leave.

'See ya,' Isaac shot back, not even breaking my gaze to turn to look at her.

* * *

54

The second day was a little easier. Corridors started to look less identical to each other. Isaac working his magic on my maths clearly impressed Mr Jordan, because while he didn't smile at me, he didn't frown either. And I had lunch with a few students who seemed nice enough to kill time with. But the best part of my day was that Thomas wasn't around because he was away playing a rugby fixture.

Yesterday his attention had been flattering. Even if he was a bit awkward, he was tall and handsome and friendly, and I'd seen the way other girls had been watching him eat lunch with me; he was clearly popular at Thornton's. It had been flattering to have attention from two of the most-liked boys in the school, even if the butterflies that had gone wild when Isaac touched my hand didn't so much as flutter when I'd eaten lunch with Thomas. But things had changed last night. My instinct hadn't stopped yapping since I'd searched through my blazer pocket and not been able to find Isaac's note. I was sure Thomas had taken it. Something wasn't right there.

And it was as if thinking about him made him appear.

'Cynthia! I've been wanting to catch up with you,' Thomas exclaimed, half jogging so he arrived at my locker the same time I did.

'Thomas.' I smiled but stepped back a bit. He was so tall that he towered over me, and I didn't like the feeling of standing between him and the lockers.

'Please excuse the attire.' He gestured his hand down his chest and torso, proudly encouraging me to look at the rugby kit he was wearing.

'Ah, no worries, I've seen worse.' I shrugged. 'Sup?' I asked, eager to move on to my next lesson.

'Firstly, I wanted to make sure that your second day was progressing without hiccups, and secondly, I wanted to invite you to a—'

'Party at your house on Saturday?' I interjected, finishing his sentence for him.

He tipped his head quizzically.

'Isaac told me,' I shot back, searching his eyes for a glint of annoyance.

Like an Oscar-winning actor, he didn't miss a beat. 'Of course he did!' He grinned, but the smile didn't entirely reach his emerald eyes. 'Perfect. It would be nice to have you and your family there. This party is always one of the most anticipated of the year.' He shrugged, clearly not caring that he was coming across as braggadocious.

'Umm, yeah, great. Not sure if my dad will let me come though.' I wasn't entirely sure I wanted to go to this party. Even with the draw of Isaac being there, there was something about Thomas that was making me uneasy.

Swiftly, he used his arm to create a barrier between the locker and the corridor.

If I was anyone else, I guess I would have flinched but the south London in me took two quick steps back, like a champion boxer ready to defend themselves.

'You know, Cynthia, I think Isaac is developing a bit of a thing for you.'

I wasn't expecting that. And nor was my usually quick mouth. 'Is it? That's mad still.' I hadn't yet worked out how to manage my south London twang when caught off guard.

'Yeah, and to be honest, I don't blame him.' He smiled.

The loud ring of the bell that announced it was time for next period was a welcome interruption.

'I'll text you the party details,' Thomas confirmed. In that moment an unruly patch of hair fell forwards on to his face in a way that made him look completely different. Less mature, perhaps. Less certain of himself. 'All you have to do is show up.' He smiled brightly again. 'Gotta run; student council meeting.'

I watched him long enough to catch him turning back to look at me one last time before he turned the corner.

CHAPTER SEVEN

'I just don't get it, J. This is all a bit mad, innit? Like some *Twilight* shit, two boys both after me?' I laughed.

It was later that evening and I was sprawled on my bed, talking to Jadell on the phone. Outside, it was getting dark. Mum had called to say that she was running late but that she'd left dinner in the oven.

'Yeah, but it's also a good distraction, Cyn. Like, you've been through a lot. It's time you let your hair down. And I mean that fi true.' She cackled.

'Girl, shut up!' I hollered through giggles. 'Leave me and my 4C bundles alone, thank you. We can't all be picture-perfect every day.' I sighed, turning to look at myself in the mirror on my dressing table. I roughly pulled off the green scrunchie that was trying, albeit unsuccessfully, to control my frizzy bun and let out a sigh of relief. 'Speaking of hair, if I do go to the party on Saturday, what am I gonna do with it?'

'Braids?' J offered. 'Although if you don't get them done like, tomorrow, you'll be cutting it fine. They won't have time to settle.'

Braids took at least five days to loosen up on both your scalp and brain. Also, braids would mean having to see Auntie Jackie. I would rather run naked across the fields at Thornton's than spend time with her.

'Not enough time,' I agreed.

'OK, new idea – and hear me out before you say anything,' Jadell began. 'I know you've always been anti-creamy crack, but perming your hair would make it so much easier to manage—'

'Gurrrrrl,' I sang in hushed tones as I used my fingers like an afro pick, pulling the digits through my coily hair. I knew she was right. Straight hair was easier to manage – or at least that's what we Black girls and women had been told – but I'd seen the dark sides to chemical straightening. 'I don't know, man, look what happened to Nicole. You know, the one that was in 9C? One minute she had a head full of hair and then next thing it was like she had alopecia.'

'Jesus, yeah, that was deep,' Jadell agreed. 'You know what, on a real, who am I to tell you what to do? I know my hair causes me less headache just because. I love your hair how it is. Why don't you just wear it natural?'

See, that's why J was a real one. She understood her privileges. And in a society that was only now trying to unlearn everything and admit how some had it harder than others just because of how they looked, I rated Jadell for always keeping it 100.

'Thanks,' I sighed, flopping down on the bed.

'So anyway, tell me more about Mr Hayes,' Jadell prompted. That was her new nickname for Isaac. Both our parents would often play music from back in the day and one of their favourites was a guy called Isaac Hayes. A memory came flooding back to me: the last time we'd listened to his music as a family.

* * *

59

We were in our old house. The kitchen there had massive skylights that allowed the light to come pouring in and cover us like a warm bath. It was Sunday morning and Mike and I were sitting at the kitchen table, busying ourselves with homework, while Mum prepared pancakes. I frowned as Dad started playing another song from the last century and I asked why we couldn't ever listen to anything made this decade.

'You kids just don't know what a classic sounds like,' my dad said, but he was smiling as he turned up the volume and grabbed my mum by the waist, twirling her around the kitchen, pancake batter from her whisk flying through the air. Over the sound of the music and Mum's laughter, there was a ping from Mike's phone.

PING

PING

PING

PI—

He grabbed it and silenced it.

'Girl trouble, eh?' Mum joked, glancing at him.

'They won't leave me alone,' he said, smiling. But I could tell the smile was forced. His brow knitted together as he looked down at the messages, as if what he was reading annoyed him. Or maybe scared him. He quickly turned the phone face down.

'You know what? I'm gonna go find somewhere quiet to study.'

'That's my boy!' Dad encouraged, now fussing with the coffee machine.

Mike scooped up his books, grabbed his phone and left the room.

'Ah, I hope he isn't putting too much pressure on himself,' Mum whispered into the air once he'd left.

'Aht aht,' Dad began. 'It's pressure that makes diamonds, V. He is

60

destined for great things. Now is not the time for him to slack. He will be fine.' Dad moved back towards her and squeezed the back of her neck.

I gently rubbed my own neck now.

'Oh, J, he is just nice, innit. Today he opened up a little more. He told me his dad died of cancer when he was two. And his mum's dead as well.'

'Oh, rah, so he ain't untouched then,' she mused.

Untouched was the word we used for people who hadn't yet lost someone they loved. Jadell's favourite aunt died a few years before Mike did. And to be honest her aunt came like her mum. She raised Jadell when her own mum was out . . . doing stuff. It had been cancer too. She went so quickly. I still remember how frail she was the last time I saw her. Jadell hasn't been the same since but, I mean, who is after you lose someone like that? Some say she's gone off the rails but she's my girl and I'm gonna stick beside her. Plus, when Big Mike died, she held it down. Answered every call. Understood what I meant when I said I felt haunted. And really tried to get me to see it from my parents' point of view when I was mad vex we were leaving ends.

From my bedroom window I saw the flash of my mum's car headlights as she pulled into the drive.

'Listen, my mum is back, I gotta go.' I yawned and, with a promise to text tomorrow with any updates, I hung up. To be honest, I was happy someone was home. This new house was far bigger than our home in London. Being surrounded by sprawling fields was nice during the day when it was busy with dog-walkers and kids playing, but being in the middle of so much nothingness became creepy after the sun set. I took one last look at myself in the mirror, considering my hair, still undecided about what to do with it for the party, before heading downstairs. I could already hear Mum busying herself in the hallway.

It wasn't until I was halfway down the staircase that I realised it wasn't Mum at all. Whoever this person was, they had hair that fell to the middle of their back.

'Hello?' I asked, shocked to hear in my own voice that the fear I was feeling had come out as pure aggression.

'Hey, baby!' the person exclaimed as they turned to face me.

Shit. It *was* Mum after all. What the hell had she done to her hair?

I stood rooted to the spot with what must have been a shocked expression on my face. She immediately started explaining.

'Oh, Cyn, I just needed a change. Do you like it? Your aunt wanted me to go even longer but I had to tell her, listen, I'm not one of those young girls on social media! What do you think of the colour? I went with 1B as I feel like it made it look more natural,' she rattled on, not giving me time to answer one question before she went on to the next.

Slowly, I came down to the bottom of the stairs. For as long as I had been alive, I had *never* seen my mother with this much hair. When relatives were a little tipsy at family functions the story about Mum coming home from school when she was seventeen with her head shaved always came up.

'She gave me the shock of my life. I honestly thought she needed sectioning. A head full of good hair, just gone,' my

62

grandmother would grumble once the rum had loosened her tongue. I came from a family that believed a woman's beauty was tied to her hair – particularly how much of it she had. I'd always seen the fact that Mum had gone against that grain as inspirational, a sincere two fingers up to all that Black girls and women were expected to be. Seeing her with hair on her head not only shocked me, it worried me. Not that it looked bad, it just . . . wasn't her.

But I could see by the look in her eyes that she was looking for emotional back-up, a sign that she had done the right thing. Given all she had been through the last couple of years, it was the least I could do.

I fixed a smile to my face.

'Wow, Mum! Is that you? Yeah, it looks so good!' I cried.

Her eyes lit with joy.

'Really?' she asked, flicking some of the hair behind her shoulder. 'It's not too much?'

The thing was, as much as I couldn't stand Auntie Jackie, the one thing she could do was lay a frontal. There wasn't a single hair out of place on this unit. The colour and style made Mum look even younger. Honestly, it looked great – it would just take some getting used to.

'Yeah, it's wicked,' I said, trying not to let my concern show.

'I just felt like trying something new, you know, Cyn? A little refreshment. Anyways, come help me with this shopping so I can get sorted before your dad comes home,' she ordered.

As I scooped up the shopping bags and followed her into the kitchen, I wondered what Dad would think when he did get home. Not that it should have mattered. But when times were lighter, he'd always boasted that her shaved head was one of the things that attracted him to her.

'Do you know how self-assured a Black woman has to be to shave off her hair?' he would ask rhetorically. 'I love that your mum doesn't hide behind the hair of an Indian or Brazilian. She allows her true beauty to shine through!' he'd say.

I guess we would have to wait and see.

Given that Mum was enamoured with her new style and happily veg-prepping, I saw this as a perfect time to do some preparation of my own. After talking it through with Jadell, I'd decided the draw of Isaac was more than enough to make up for having to potentially spend more time with Thomas. I wanted to go to this party.

'Mum, some of my new friends at Thornton's have invited me to their home for a party at the weekend.'

Before I'd even finished, I saw her pleasant expression turn stoic.

'Please, hear me out,' I went on before she could say anything. 'Their parents will be there, and I promise to stay glued to my phone. Please, please, can I go?' I begged, leaning over the kitchen island in desperation. I'd decided not to mention that she and Dad were invited. Even if it would make it more likely that Mum would say yes, I didn't think I could survive the embarrassment of Dad grilling every boy he saw there about his intentions towards me.

'Oh, Cynthia,' she sighed, making my name last about thirty seconds and I knew she was preparing herself to say no. Since Mike had died, both Mum and Dad had become like the FBI, keeping track of my location. In the last two years, I had done almost nothing but go from home to school and back.

I felt my shoulders grow tense with annoyance. Anger even. And, though I was embarrassed to admit it, most of my anger was towards Mike. If he hadn't argued with Dad and then decided to make his own way back from university that night, none of this would be happening. I would still be in my home, surrounded by the friends I knew and loved and living the life of a normal teenage girl. Instead, here I was standing in a kitchen in the middle of mookoland, begging to go to a party where adults would be present.

'I really want to let you go,' she said softly, clearly aware that I was getting worked up. 'But . . .' She trailed off.

'Mum, don't. Don't do that. You come home looking like a whole new woman, saying you fancy a change. What about me? Doesn't anyone think I deserve a change too?' My voice cracked.

'Oh, baby girl,' she hushed as she came towards me. 'I get it, I get it.' She pulled me in for a hug and I felt myself melt into her.

'No, you don't,' I said, the anger rising again.

'I do,' she said firmly, pulling back so now she was looking up at me. 'Do you think I want to keep you imprisoned? Do you think I want to be the one who doesn't allow you to live your life? I'm *scared*, Cynthia. Your brother was the most perfect boy and look what happened.' A small sob escaped her. 'I can't have that happen again,' she finished, so quietly that I could barely hear her.

'But I'm not him, Mum. I'm not Mike.' My anger had melted as suddenly as it had come, and now I could feel the pressure of tears behind my eyes too. Her brown eyes seemed to be searching my face for something but I wasn't sure what. Her son, perhaps?

She released her grip on me and went back to the sink. 'I know you're not.' The crack in her voice let me know she was fully crying now. 'And you're right, it's not fair.' She took a deep breath, turning to face me once more. 'Yes, you can go – but your father or I will drop you off and pick you up. I want you to call us at the first sign of trouble. And if I have even the slightest reason to suspect nonsense, Cynthia Princess Adegoke, I promise you won't leave this house until you get married. Do I make myself clear?'

I hated my middle name, but in that moment I was too happy to care. I bounded over and hugged her so forcefully she had to steady herself on the sink. 'Oh, thank you, thank you, thank you!' I said, joyfully dancing around the kitchen.

'So is anyone going to let me know why we are expressing such tremendous gratitude?' Dad's voice startled us both.

'Lord in Heaven, Tunde, you almost put me in an early grave,' Mum said, clutching her chest for effect.

I watched Dad's gaze grow wide as he saw Mum's new hairdo. I almost felt the temperature in the room drop. He hated it.

'Mum said I could go to a party on Saturday!' I announced before he could comment on her hair. I watched Dad's chest puff as he readied himself to overrule her and quickly went on. 'It's at Thomas Goddard's. You know, the head boy, who you met the other day? Yeah, him. His parents are big donors to the school and apparently they throw an annual party.' I was really playing it up, knowing full well that everything I said was right up Dad's street. I saw the fight in him dissipate almost immediately.

'Hmm. Very well then,' he said, placing his briefcase on the kitchen island. I could almost feel Mum squirm as she looked at his case. She hated anything she deemed as 'outside things' near where we ate or slept. 'But I will drop you off and pick you up, no exceptions,' he added, clearly trying to redeem himself as head of the household.

'Thanks, Dad,' I said, trying to suppress my smile, already planning on texting Jadell an update as soon as he left the room.

'Veronica, I shall now retire until dinner time,' he announced.

Mum flicked her hair back, clearly in the hopes that he would now acknowledge it, but he turned to leave the kitchen without another word.

'Darling, what do you think of my hair?' she sang after him, before he was out of earshot. There was a desperation in her voice that almost made me feel embarrassed for her.

He paused and looked back at her briefly from the doorway. 'Playing with your physical appearance won't bring him back, Veronica,' he said solemnly, before leaving the kitchen entirely, a sad silence in his wake.

CHAPTER EIGHT

SEND ME A PIC!

I read Jadell's message and then threw the phone back on the bed. It was the afternoon of the party and I had spent so much time and energy on my hair that I realised only now that I'd completely neglected to plan my outfit.

My bedroom floor resembled the changing room of a fast-fashion outlet during a sale. With just two hours before Dad was due to drop me off, I was on the brink of sweating out my edges due to how many times I had changed my clothes. I had tried to video-call with Jadell so she could help, but she was out with Amanda, another one of our friends. By *friend* I mean someone who was part of the group who I didn't really check for, and by *our* I mean Jadell's. Amanda always gave off sly jealous vibes, like what she really wanted was to be Jadell's number one, but she couldn't because Jadell and I had been besties since nursery, so I took the title by default. I knew that the moment my back was turned, she would try and take my spot and so said, so done. Luckily, J and I were texting so she couldn't hear the immediate lump that rose in my throat when she told me who she was with.

'Get a grip, Cyn,' I said aloud to myself.

I walked over to my window and grabbed one of Mike's crystals off the windowsill. I had taken a few more from one of the boxes of his stuff that was sitting in what would have been his room. Mum must have clocked, because whenever she tidied my room, she would arrange them as if they were on show in a shop. But thankfully she didn't ask me about them. I didn't want to tell anyone because I knew I would sound silly, but I believed there was a part of those rocks that held his energy. And now, more than ever, I wanted to believe that part of him was here to encourage me.

I flopped down on the bed next to my phone, but abruptly got up again when I remembered my hair. There was no way I was going to mess it up. After less cajoling than I'd expected, Mum had been convinced to drive me to an afro hairdresser's I'd found online. I secretly think she was grateful for my research as she needed someone to keep her hair looking good too now. The place was over an hour away, but it had great reviews. I decided to get a silk press, which would free me from the tyranny of my 4C afro but wasn't as permanent as chemically straightening my hair. Perhaps it was because they were outside of London but the hairdressers were on time, friendly and professional – even Mum was shocked.

When they spun my chair around and I was able to look in the mirror, I hardly recognised myself. My now straightened hair fell way past my shoulders and the thickness and shine would have made anyone think it was a weave.

'What healthy hair you have, babe,' cooed the young

hairdresser. I couldn't help but flick it. 'Now, don't forget, try not to sweat too much, don't get it wet, tie it down at night and don't fuss with it. I can tell you're going to struggle with that last one,' she said, laughing.

And she was right. Since I'd got home, I'd fussed with it ten thousand ways. It was a revelation to me. Even Dad had said it looked nice. A compliment from him these days felt like seeing a pig fly.

Now, as I lay awkwardly on my bed, I chastised myself for not putting the same effort beforehand into what I was going to wear. I held my phone aloft and messaged the one person who could help. Isaac.

> Hey, what you wearing?

Before I had a chance to put my arm down, I could see he was typing a response. Since he had put his number in my phone on my second day at school, we had been in contact pretty much non-stop every evening, first just texting about maths homework but quickly moving on to talking about everything. At school the vibe was a bit different. In my classes, I was having to focus so hard to keep up that I didn't have space to think about anything else, and during lunch and free time, Thomas always seemed to be hanging around. Isaac had a wall up when Thomas was there, like he didn't want Thomas to know we were becoming friends. But away from school, we were talking constantly. Every time his name popped up on my screen, I felt a swooping in my stomach. And his name was popping up *a lot*. The speed of his responses could win gold at the Texting Olympics.

> Right now?

I felt my face grow hot. His next message came half a second later.

> LOL JK

I sent a laughter emoji in response and then waited as I could see he was typing again.

> Jeans, white trainers and pullover probably

I felt my face grow tight at the word pullover. Who said *pullover*? I was almost sure that was a word he'd got from the Goddards.

> Cyn, don't stress. You'll look good in whatever

The swooping sensation shot through my stomach and around my heart this time. I stood up and rifled through the mound of clothes on the floor. I would wear what I'd tried on first, which

71

was a black dress with a white T-shirt underneath, black chunky boots and a leather jacket.

I heard my phone vibrate again.

> Besides, Thomas is wearing a three-piece suit. LOL

I giggled even though I wasn't sure if he was joking.

'Cynthia, I'll be in the car,' Dad called up from downstairs.

That was my cue to not keep him waiting. I took one last look at myself in the mirror. While the outfit wasn't going to win me any best-dressed awards, I felt comfortable and, with my hair like it was, I thought I looked pretty good.

I took a quick selfie and fired it off to Jadell before grabbing a small bag and hurrying down the stairs.

Dad had already started the engine.

I took a deep breath and sank into the passenger seat, willing the trip to be a lot quicker than the estimated forty-five minutes I had spotted on the satnav.

As soon as we drove off, he started in. 'I trust that you will put your best foot forward tonight,' he said.

What did he even mean by that?

'I'm sure you understand who the Goddards are,' he added, as if he could hear my thoughts, 'and how making a good impression on them could be beneficial to all of us.'

I let out a sigh. In his mind this party was more about him than me. It was about us being accepted in this community. 'Yes, *sir*,' I responded sarcastically. I saw his grip on the wheel became extra-tight and knew I was pushing it. Not that he would ever hit me. Dad had never once spanked me or Mike. I knew lots of kids in my school were hit, but Dad had been raised in a household governed by the constant threat of physical pain and he said he would never do that to us. He punished us with sharp words instead.

I sighed and gazed out of the window. We were moving at such speed, it felt as though every field we whizzed past blended into the one before it, just an endless scene of varying greens. As if hypnotised, I remembered the last time all three of us were in the car together, when Dad and I had taken Mike back to uni after Easter break. Mum had gone to visit Nan and Auntie Jackie for the last few days of his visit, so it was just the three of us. On Friday night Dad had insisted we drop Big Mike back to university on Sunday afternoon. Initially Mike had put up a fight, saying he would rather meet up with his new friends and travel back by train. Something about this visit had been different; he seemed strained and disengaged, even barking at me a few times, which was unlike him. Mum had put it down to coursework stress, but I wasn't so sure. I think he finally conceded only when he clocked that Dad actually just missed him but didn't know how to say it.

'Errr, where do you think you're going?' Mike asked as we both jostled towards the front passenger seat.

'Ummm, to get in the car,' I said, elbowing him in the side to get him out of the way.

'Nah, Cyn, you know the pecking order.' He pushed me aside. 'It's Mum's seat first. If Mum isn't here it's mine, and only if I'm not here is it yours,' he said in the sort of tone usually reserved for toddlers.

73

I kissed my teeth. 'Things have changed. You're hardly ever here now!' I dug my heels in, trying to get back to the door handle.

'And yet today here I am.' He chuckled, tickling me so I had no choice but to take a step back to escape his hands. He then quickly opened the passenger door and fell into the front seat, slamming the door behind him.

'Mike!' I huffed.

He made a crybaby face from the window. I cussed him under my breath and regretfully slid into the back seat.

'Don't worry,' he said, looking at me in the rear-view mirror 'One day I'll be working so hard I'll have my own car and the seat will be all yours.' He winked.

'By the time someone sees you as employable, I'll be a corpse,' I snapped back, unable to control a giggle.

'So I'm talking to a ghost then?' he laughed, firing his jab back as quickly as I had given him one.

'Ooooof, that was good,' I acknowledged. 'But don't worry, it's a long drive. I'll get you back.'

'Oh, my dear baby sis,' he said, craning his neck to look at me with a sad look on his face. 'If I had to wait for you to beat me in a cussing match, I'd be the corpse.' He burst out laughing.

'Care to share the joke?' Dad asked, finally claiming his spot behind the wheel.

'Yeah, your daughter,' Mike responded quickly, laughing again.

'Aht aht, Michael,' Dad said, though I could tell he was trying hard to suppress his own laugher.

'Daaaaddddd!' I moaned.

'I'm sorry, I'm sorry,' Dad offered up, starting the car. 'Michael, don't make fun of your sister.'

'OK, sorry, Dad,' Mike said, suddenly sounding solemn. His solemnity lasted all of three seconds until they both burst out laughing again.

And moments later I joined in too.

'And what about Thomas?' Dad's question pulled me back to the present day. I noticed we were being held hostage by a red light.

I began to squirm a little in my seat.

'What about him?' I batted back, trying to ignore the growing knot in my stomach.

I could tell that Dad was uncomfortable too. 'He presented himself as a well-rounded, polite young boy. But, of course, that was in front of me and the Head. Have you found him to be nice? Not too . . . familiar?' he asked.

'Umm, yeah. Yes. I guess so. He takes his multiple school roles very seriously. He's been really helpful this week.' I noticed my voice was a little higher than usual.

'Good, good. I think he is someone you could grow a great . . . friendship with,' he said. 'Eventually.'

'Oh deffo . . . I mean definitely. His brother is great too.' I smiled. I didn't know why I'd mentioned Isaac and I chastised myself as Dad immediately jumped on it.

'Hmm. The adopted boy?' Dad's eyes quickly glanced in my direction.

I kept my expression unreadable. 'Yes,' I sighed, wishing he would just spit out what he really meant.

'You know I don't like to mince my words, Cynthia. While I appreciate the PR front of their brotherhood, he's not one of

75

them. The boy is a charity case. And only God knows where he is really from.'

'Where he's *really* from?!' I exploded, the rage rising in my chest. 'Dad, can you hear yourself? Do you know what happened on my first day? Two white girls came into the bathroom. They didn't know I was in there. They not only mocked my hair and where *I'm* from, but they also knew what happened to Michael. And guess what? They laughed. They said we "bring it on ourselves".' I was half shouting now. 'You think any of these white families want us here? They're probably saying the same things about us that you just said about Isaac!'

I must have hit a nerve as Dad didn't even notice the car in front of us stop until we were right behind it. He hit the brakes so hard I had to throw out my arms to stop myself ending up in the glovebox.

'I will not be undermined, Cynthia,' he snapped sharply, slamming his palm into the steering wheel. 'Boys like that are no good. And before you try to point out the obvious, Michael was different. *We* are different,' he fumed. He was shaking with anger.

I wanted so badly to give him the tongue-lashing I'd been wishing Mum would give him. I wanted him to understand that there was no 'us and them' – to the white families, we all looked the same. I wanted him to know that uprooting me from south London to the middle of nowhere wouldn't change the fact that we're Black, and it wouldn't bring his son back either. I wanted to say it all.

But I also really wanted to see Isaac. And I knew my dad

well enough to know when he was at the end of his tether. So, I didn't push it any further.

We sat in silence for the rest of the drive.

CHAPTER NINE

Thirty minutes of uncomfortable silence later, we arrived at the Goddards'. Turning into the drive, we made our way up a long, winding path, finally arriving at a set of large black iron gates. As Dad inched the car closer, they slowly opened up, allowing us to continue through. The path continued to twist and turn until the trees around it fell away and the view opened up ahead of us.

'Jeez.' I exhaled, unable to hide how impressed I was. The Goddards' house – actually, *house* didn't cut it; their *estate* – looked twice the size of Thornton's. I would never in my life have guessed that this was a single-family home.

Dad let out a low, soft whistle. Even he was blown away.

The road had opened out into a circular patch of land with a water fountain at the centre. Framing that were many cars, at least thirty, all of which looked brand new. And expensive.

Seemingly out of nowhere, a short white man, who looked to be in his early forties, appeared, dressed in what looked like a butler's uniform. He took off his hat and used it to flag Dad down.

He waited for Dad to wind the window down before speaking.

'Welcome, Mr Adegoke. Allow me to take care of your

car while you attend the party.'

Him knowing our family name didn't shock me – Thomas's personality had given me enough clues to know his parents would like to ensure every box was checked . . . but a valet? I slowly reached up and touched my face just to make sure my eyeballs were still firmly in their sockets. I thought this was something that only existed in American sitcoms.

'Well, I was just going to drop my daughter off . . .' Dad began.

'Please, trust that your vehicle will be in good hands,' the valet advised with a smile.

'I suppose I could come in for a short time.' While Dad's tone suggested he wanted to act as if he was doing them a favour, the small smile creeping across his lips proved otherwise.

Shit. There went my plan of keeping Dad well away from my social life.

'Miss Adegoke,' the man said, as he approached my door and opened it.

I stepped out, realising to my horror that I'd begun to sweat through my silk slip dress – and it was now super wrinkled too.

'Great,' I muttered under my breath, drawing the sides of my leather jacket together to try and hide the sweat patches. Even next to the man who was about to park our car, I felt terribly underdressed.

Dad handed over the keys and then came to stand beside me.

'If you both head up the stairs, you'll be met by Samuel, who will show you to the main house. Have a wonderful evening.' He jumped into the driver's seat and left us standing at the base of the steps.

The main house? I thought to myself. *How many buildings were there? And what were the others? Servants' quarters?* My head was officially spinning.

'Well, this is quite something,' Dad admitted, turning on his heel to do a quick sweep of the surroundings.

'Mmmhmm,' I muttered.

As much as Dad liked to act the bigshot, I could tell even he felt self-conscious here.

We climbed a set of stone stairs that led us to a pathway lined by beautiful rose bushes. Twisting through them were strands of soft white twinkling lights, illuminating the way. It was like something out of a fairy tale. As the valet had advised, at the end of this path was Samuel, a tall man who wore a tuxedo and a bright smile. He looked older than fifty but there was a handsome youthfulness still visible in his tanned face.

'Miss Adegoke,' he greeted me. 'It's a pleasure to finally meet you. Both of the Goddard boys have done nothing but sing your praises since you joined Thornton's.' He beamed, unaware that he was perhaps giving me more information than 'the boys' wanted me to be privy to.

'Is that so?' Dad cut in, unable to hide the grin appearing on his face.

'Why, yes, she's made quite an impression. We may be looking at a duel for her heart if things continue this way!' He laughed heartily and gave me a wink.

I felt my stomach do somersaults as I clocked Dad's smile starting to fade.

Samuel seemed to notice it too. 'And, Mr Adegoke, I

understand you're doing incredible work at the city hospital,' he added quickly.

A few minutes of boring conversation about his role at the hospital and Dad was beaming once more. This Samuel guy was good.

'Right, let me not keep you,' he said finally. 'Do follow me.'

And we followed Samuel to the right, towards the sound of music and chatter. As we came around the corner, the view opened up to reveal a sprawling garden, framing the biggest house I had ever seen.

As I was gawping at the house, a tall white man approached us and Samuel quickly whispered in his ear. They were the same height and seemed to be of a similar age, but this other man radiated privilege and wealth. When he turned to look at us, the sharp glint in his emerald eyes immediately gave him away.

'Mr Adegoke, it's such a pleasure to finally meet you. Thomas Goddard Senior,' he said, putting out his hand.

'Likewise, likewise,' my father responded, meeting Mr Goddard's outstretched hand with his own.

'And you must be the famous Cynthia,' Mr Goddard said, turning to me with a smile.

I shuffled uncomfortably from one foot to the other. 'Famous?' I asked.

'Oh yes! The way both my boys sing your praises, anyone would think they go to school with Marcus Rashford,' he said.

Dad's chest got visibly higher.

'Oh, cool,' I said, feeling more and more uncomfortable under his scrutiny.

'Speaking of my sons, Cynthia, I think the boys are in the

games room with the other young people. Samuel, would you be so gracious as to escort Cynthia there? She must be bored sick of us adults,' he said, giving a chuckle and nudging Dad like they were old friends.

'Of course. Miss Adegoke, please follow me this way,' Samuel instructed, stepping aside so I could go in front of him.

As desperate as I was to escape this conversation, leaving Dad unattended felt dangerous.

'Umm, Dad, what time will you be back for me?' I asked, hoping to remind him that he hadn't been planning on staying. But Mr Goddard had other ideas.

'Back?' Mr Goddard asked, aghast. 'You're not leaving already, are you, Mr Adegoke? I'd love to introduce you to my wife Clementine before you go, at least.'

'I'd be honoured,' Dad said with a small nod of his head. 'And please, call me Tunde,' he added. He was clearly overjoyed at being asked to stay. I quickly forced a smile, hoping it would hide my dismay. Not only did I feel super self-conscious about my outfit choice, but now it looked as if Dad was going to act as my chaperone. *Great.*

As it seemed like there was no other option, I gave Dad and Mr Goddard an awkward wave goodbye and let Samuel guide me towards the enormous house.

'Call me if you need me, dear!' Dad called after me.

Dear? I thought. He had never, ever called me that. In fact, I couldn't remember when he'd last used any term of endearment for me. I rolled my eyes, knowing he couldn't see.

'Parents, eh?' Samuel said knowingly, already a lot more relaxed in both body language and tone now that he was out of earshot of his boss. Meanwhile, I was only growing even more nervous. Aside from my connection with Isaac, I felt as if I hadn't gotten off to the right start at Thornton's. I didn't feel settled and hadn't yet met a group of friends that made me feel as secure as Jadell and others did at St Martin's. Going into a party with all the Thornton's kids and their long-established friendship cliques suddenly seemed about the worst idea imaginable, but I tried to shake the feeling off.

Samuel led me through a set of grand glass-panelled doors into the kitchen, which looked like one that Mum would have sold her left arm for. It was massive and yet, somehow, it still felt homely. Off-white cabinets accented with gold handles. Marble worktops. An island that could have comfortably accommodated at least fifteen people. In the middle of the island was a cooker with a collection of shiny pots and pans hanging from above. I sneakily glanced in them to check my reflection. Thankfully, my hair was still playing fair, but I was worried about how long that would last with all this nervous sweating.

'There's a service kitchen, otherwise this wouldn't look quite so pristine,' Samuel said, giving me another wink, clearly aware that I was studying everything.

I didn't want to embarrass myself by asking what a service kitchen was, so I made a mental note to look it up later. On the far side of the kitchen was an imposing round table in what seemed to be the same material as the kitchen worktops. It looked as if it were about to buckle underneath the weight of all the flowers on it. Breath-taking bunches of roses and peonies (Mum's favourite) burst forth from vases that looked like they belonged in a museum rather than a family home.

Behind them, through a wide doorway, I clocked an all-white living room, peppered with a few people. The glimpse I caught made me feel even more underdressed. A lady perched on the arm of the sofa closest to me was wearing a velvet evening gown. I folded my arms across my body again.

A ringing came from Samuel's pocket.

'Miss Adegoke, please wait here. I won't be a moment,' he promised as he fished his phone out of his pocket and stepped outside to answer it.

I was grateful for the alone time, even if it was only for a few moments. My head was spinning, and I desperately wanted to message Jadell. I looked over my shoulder, checking that the coast was clear. Samuel was still on his phone on the other side of the glass doors. I whipped out my phone and started typing:

> GIRL THIS PLACE IS MAD
> IT'S BASICALLY A PALACE
> THERE WAS SUM1 2 PARK THE CAR
> NOW A BUTLER IS

'EXCUSE ME!' A shrill cry came from my left, nearly making me drop my phone.

I turned to see a petite white woman in a green silk dress, staring at me angrily.

'I don't think you're being paid to faff about on your phone. I suggest you get back to the kitchen and bring out some more canapés,' she sneered. 'And if you could be bothered, I'll take a glass of champagne too – chilled, please, *unlike* the last one I was given,' she finished haughtily.

It took a few seconds for me to register what was going on. And once I did, once I realised that she'd mistaken me for *the help*, I wasn't sure whether to laugh or cry. But just as I went to respond, the sound of Samuel's voice intervened.

'Mrs Bowles, how can I help you?' he asked, and although he sounded perfectly polite, I heard a coolness in his tone that hadn't been there before.

'Well, Samuel, please tell me you will inform the Goddards how poorly the staff are behaving this year. I just found *this* one on her phone,' she said, giving me a nasty look.

I felt my hands ball into fists, the lump in my throat dissolving into anger. *Samuel had better handle this*, I thought. If not, this woman was going to end up sleeping with the fishes, as Jadell would often say of anyone who crossed her.

He smiled tightly and sighed. 'Of course, Mrs Bowles, I will let them know. However, this young lady isn't a member of staff, but actually a guest and a close schoolfriend of the Goddard boys. Her name is Cynthia Adegoke.' His tone was cool and sharp, like that of a blade.

We both watched as all the colour drained from her face.

'Oh . . . oh my, please do forgive me. I think I've had a little too much to drink,' she said with a forced laugh. Auntie Jackie always said that whenever a white woman said or did something racist, she'd often blame her shenanigans on too much wine. I didn't agree with Auntie Jackie on much, but on this she was in fact one hundred per cent correct.

'Now, Miss Adegoke, please follow me,' Samuel said, turning

to me with a real smile this time. I could tell that it was an order, and it was one that I was more than willing to follow. As we left the woman and the kitchen behind and entered a long hallway, I opened my mouth to thank him, but then I decided against it. He did what any decent person should have. Thanking him would have felt like I was apologising for my existence.

'Please be careful. This staircase is a little steep,' he advised as he opened a door at the end of the corridor. Immediately the sound of loud music and familiar voices rose towards us.

I took a deep breath before descending into the semi-darkness.

CHAPTER TEN

It felt as if we were heading into a dungeon. If it hadn't been for Thomas's familiar laughter, which I could hear floating up to us, I would have turned and made a run for it because I had seen enough true crime to know that going down into the basement is where it all goes wrong. And I don't play that. That's why Black people run first in horror films.

Soon we were nearing the bottom of the steep staircase. I quickly tried to smooth my hair with my palm and hoped to God that by now the sweat patches on my dress had faded. My mouth was dry. My hands shaky. I was panicking. What if I said something silly?

Relax! I told myself. *Breathe.*

I barely had a moment to peep at the surroundings because Thomas was already at the bottom of the stairs, looking up as if he had sensed us.

'Thank you, Samuel,' Thomas said, as if he was collecting a pizza he'd ordered.

'It's never a bother, young man.' He turned to me. 'Cynthia, it's been a pleasure.' And with that, Samuel scurried away.

I took a moment to look around the room. There was a pool table, air hockey and foosball, two enormous sofas and a huge TV mounted on the wall. This was no horror movie basement.

Cabinets and bookshelves lined the entire room, painted in a rich navy that made me feel like I was inside a cocoon. Their brass knobs and handles gave the room a luxurious feel. Expensive-looking patterned rugs were scattered around, partially covering the pale wood floors. On paper it shouldn't have all worked, but somehow the rugs tied the entire space together. The few bits of free wall space were decorated with more art, though these pieces were less abstract and more fun than the ones upstairs. There were a bunch of other kids in the room but only one face I recognised – Molly's. She gave a half-hearted smile when my eyes met hers. I didn't bother to return it. I might have been in need of new friends, but I wasn't *that* desperate. My heart sank as I realised there was no sign of Isaac.

'I'm so thrilled you could make it,' Thomas said, drawing my attention back to him. Isaac hadn't been joking when he'd told me Thomas would be wearing a suit. Well, a shirt and trousers. And a bow tie. If I hadn't known he was my age, I would have guessed he was in his twenties.

'Hiya,' I said, more shyly than I intended.

'Wow, your hair. It's so straight. So nice,' he said.

I kept an eye on his hands to make sure he wasn't going to try and touch it. If he had, my attempt to make a good impression would have gone out the window, right after his arm, because I would have karate-chopped it off.

'Thanks,' I said, once I was sure my hair was safe. I thought I heard Molly snigger. I hated that girl. I could feel her eyes on me.

'You don't look so bad yourself,' I giggled, playfully flicking his bow tie. The way his eyes came alive made me regret it instantly. I'd hoped to piss Molly off, but I didn't want him getting the wrong idea.

'Really?' he asked, his voice low. I could tell his doubt was genuine and it made me soften towards him. For all his supposed confidence, it seemed like he had insecurities too. 'Dad always says "dress how you want to be addressed" but I'd much rather be more relaxed like Isaac is,' he admitted, roughly pulling at his bow tie.

My heart gave a little jump at the mention of Isaac's name, but I didn't want to seem too eager. 'Yeah, I can't imagine him in that,' I lied, because that's exactly what I was doing. I hid my smile at the thought of Isaac in a bow tie. 'Where is Isaac anyway?' I asked with forced casualness, hoping that I wasn't giving anything away.

'Knowing him, he'll be in his room. Parties aren't really his thing.'

'Not surprising,' said a short white boy who'd been listening to our conversation. I thought his name was Henry. 'The way his childhood was? My mum says foster kids will always be a bit strange. You can't have a bad start like that and expect them to grow up normal.'

I saw Thomas flush red. 'I think what Henry is trying to say is that Isaac and I had very different childhoods. No doubt it's created different strengths and weaknesses for us both,' he said weakly.

I was too stunned to speak, so instead I just nodded.

'Would you like a drink?' Thomas asked, clearly trying to change the subject. 'I can have someone bring something down from the service kitchen,' he offered, reaching towards an intercom system, complete with a video feed of the hallway upstairs. That explained why he'd been at the bottom of the stairs. He must have seen us coming.

'Gosh, yes, please. A drink would be great.' Being offered a drink reminded me of how thirsty I actually was. 'Also, what's a service kitchen?'

I'd asked quietly, but obviously not quietly enough, as Molly started giggling and I could immediately tell she was laughing at me. I instantly regretted not waiting to google it later on my phone. Thomas glanced over his shoulder to see the source of the laughter and Molly quickly pretended to be chatting to one of her friends. He turned back to me.

'It's just the kitchen we use for gatherings and parties,' he said kindly. 'The kitchen Samuel would have escorted you through is the family kitchen. That's the one we use day to day.'

'OK, got it. We only have the one kitchen,' I said loudly, trying to show that I wasn't bothered.

'Man, that sucks,' Henry piped up again. 'Sharing a kitchen with the staff must be hardcore.'

I couldn't tell if he was joking or not, but I didn't bother to explain the obvious. All of a sudden, I just wanted a moment to myself.

'The toilet, where is it?' I asked.

'Oh, let me show—' Thomas began.

'I don't need a guide, just directions,' I said, the words sharper than I'd meant them to be. If he was caught off guard by my change in attitude, he didn't show it.

He took a massive bite of his own sandwich and chewed meticulously before answering.

'Sort of. Of course, they didn't say it outright but, yeah, I've been having elocution lessons since I began living with them. Mum – Mrs Goddard – she couldn't stand the way I talked,' he said. 'Ya get me, fam?' he added sarcastically.

I laughed. I wanted to know more, how it had been when he first came here, what his world was like before he arrived at the Goddards', if we'd known the same places, maybe even some of the same people back in London. I especially wanted to know about his family. How did he even end up in the care system? Was there no one who could have taken him in? I wanted to know *everything*. But I also knew it might get deep and I didn't want to pry. I wanted him to feel comfortable with me first.

'You're the first person I've really felt comfortable with in years,' he admitted, as if he was reading my mind. 'The first person I can be myself with.'

'Do you never see your biological family? Your . . . brother?' I asked, trying not to sound nosy, but at the same time eager for him to confide in me, for him to tell me about the letters I'd seen, and their recipient.

He looked away, across the field. Even from his side profile, I could see the pain in his eyes. 'It's complicated,' he said flatly, closing up. 'What about you, Cyn? What about your family?' he asked, considerately not mentioning my brother specifically, though I felt the unspoken question.

Now it was my turn to look out across the field. It was relatively empty, which was surprising given that it was still warm, even though we were well into September. The sun swept across the grass and gently warmed every blade, making the air smell sweet, like it was still summer. My eyes danced across the space to the back of the school building. It was as grand as the front. Even a maths professor would tire of counting all the windows. At the corner of the field was the sports shed, where the teams dumped their kit so they wouldn't have to take it home every day. It was actually an old brick outhouse that could have housed a family of six. In the distance, there were a few bodies engaging in a friendly game of football, and to the edge of the field there was a group of girls having a picnic. Their light giggles travelled through the air. No one seemed to care about us.

'It's complicated too,' I said finally, quickly glancing at him. His face was warm, open, non-judgemental. 'My parents are splitting up,' I blurted out, ignoring the generational advice of 'what happens in the house, stays in the house'.

'Rah,' he answered simply, sympathy on his face.

'Rah, indeed,' I sighed, shuffling slightly so that I could lean back against the bench a bit more.

'To be real, Mr and Mrs Goddard should have divorced years ago.' He shrugged.

'Word? I mean, really?' I asked, genuinely shocked.

He half smiled. 'Cyn, it's cool to be yourself with me,' he said.

I felt my cheeks grow warm and I nodded. Even after such a short space of time, I was so used to modulating myself at Thornton's that I'd forgotten I didn't have to do it for Isaac.

'So wha really gwarn?' I asked, as if I were speaking to Jadell.

'Is that you, yeah?' he chuckled. 'Bad gyal and that?'

'Ah, shut up, fam.' I giggled, leaning over towards him just enough so I could elbow him in the side.

At that exact moment he leaned in, and his lips met mine. I was so taken aback, I half squealed, but the meeting of our mouths swallowed the sound. Gently, his lips explored mine for a few seconds before he pulled back, smiling.

'Isaac,' I said softly, putting my now spinning head in my hands.

'I really like you, Cyn,' he admitted, nudging my chin up with his thumb, looking into my eyes earnestly.

'Really?' I asked. Meeting his gaze was too intense, so I averted my eyes, looking across the field again. A movement on the side of the pitch caught my attention. It was someone carrying a hockey stick, either just going to, or just leaving, the shed. From this distance, with the sun in my eyes, I couldn't make out who it was, but something about his height and the way he was moving made me think it was Thomas. Had he seen us? Had he seen the kiss?

'Earth to Cyn!' Isaac waved a hand in front of my face to grab my attention.

'Huh?' I responded, turning to look at him.

'Rah, if it's a no, you can just tell me, you know. I'm a big boy, I can take it.' He sighed, with an embarrassed smile.

'I'm sorry,' I stuttered, a little confused. 'I think I zoned out.' I focused my attention back on him, trying not look back towards where I thought I'd seen Thomas.

'Oh, I just wanted to know if you wanted to go out to dinner for our date, maybe this Saturday? No biggie if you don't want to. We can do something more casual. But there's this pizza place in town and it's actually pretty good. We could just get coffee – not that I actually drink that stuff – or something else though, if you want to do something more chill . . .'

He had trailed off, because I'd playfully put my hand up as if I were in a lesson.

'I would really like that,' I said. 'Dinner sounds perfect.' And my heart did a little somersault in agreement.

'Oh . . . cool,' he said, visibly relaxing and grinning at me.

And then the bell warning us to get to afternoon registration rang out in congratulations, validating my observation that when you want time to move slowly, it races along without you even noticing.

'Here, eat this quick,' he advised, giving me a packet of crisps.

'OK, OK,' I laughed, taking them, and only then remembering to look over at the sports shed again.

But when I glanced over, Thomas was nowhere to be found, which made me wonder if I had even seen him at all.

CHAPTER SEVENTEEN

Thankfully, Dad texted me mid-afternoon to tell me he could pick me up. I would much rather take his frosty attitude over being driven, quite literally, round the houses with other students I barely knew.

Apart from greeting me when I got into the car, Dad drove in silence, but that was actually preferable to our normal dynamic. I did *not* want to rehash our argument from the weekend, but luckily, he didn't seem to want to either. Whether that meant he'd accepted that I wouldn't be letting him choose who I dated, or he was just waiting for the right moment to restart the battle, I didn't know. But only in the silence of the ride did I truly realise how much I'd been performing for him before; how little I'd been allowed to be my own person. I was proud that I'd stood up for myself, and this silence felt like the final act of defiance. I was no longer scared of him. Though I had to admit, I felt a tiny bit bad too. Not only was that the first time I had ever spoken to him like that, but then his wife had interrupted to ask for a divorce. Our lives had more ups and downs than a soap opera at the moment.

In the quiet of the car, I tapped away on my phone. I hadn't been able to update Jadell with what had happened at lunch until now.

WHAT?! A DINNER DATE?
IS THAT YOU YH?!
LET ME REMIND U FRM NOW
THAT IM UR MAID OF DISHONOUR
OR WHATEVER THEY CALL IT.

I fought to hold back a giggle when I remembered the pact we had made at primary school. It was weird; even then she was 'the prettier one'. Whenever we played house or there was a game of kiss-chase that ended in a playground marriage, I was always the bridesmaid.

U KNOW DIS
WHO ELSE WILL I PICK? MOLLY?!
LOL
TALK L8R GATOR

Gator was our code for when there was someone snappy around, a signal that we needed to pick up the convo later. I can't remember who came up with it, but I was grateful for it right then as I could tell that Dad was getting annoyed with the tapping. While I wasn't afraid of his reactions any longer, that didn't mean I wanted to purposefully court his anger.

I slid my phone into my inside blazer pocket and it made a soft *clack* sound. Big Mike's crystals. There was a sudden rush of guilt as I realised I had forgotten all about them. I put my hand inside and pulled the citrine out, silently toying with it as I looked out of the window. In my reflection I could see that the roots of my hair were finally starting to revolt. One more day and I would have to go back to putting it in a bun. Maybe Mum was right, braids would be a better choice in the long run. No way in hell would they be done by Auntie Jackie though. Jadell had suggested Auntie June's place, but that would mean I would have to head into London and I just wasn't feeling it at the moment. I sighed and let my thoughts roam until the image of Thomas at the edge of the field flooded my memory. Had I been seeing things? If not, had *he* seen *us*? And how would he take it if he had? It would have been clear that I'd only let him walk me to the library to try and throw him off course.

I shook my head, feeling annoyed that I couldn't just allow myself to enjoy what had happened today. Finally, there seemed to be a shift in the energy. Nothing would bring Mike back, but I knew that he would have wanted me to keep living and enjoying my life like any other sixteen-year-old girl. I wanted to go to parties, get my hair done, talk loudly on the phone with my friends and go on dates. For so long it felt as if those happier, lighter things would never again be within reach, but now I could feel them all brushing lightly against my fingertips. And yet here came my constant doubts and fears trying to snatch them away, like death had stolen Mike away from me.

I let my head rest on the car window, and I sighed. It came out a little louder than expected, making Dad look over.

'How was school?' he asked briskly.

'Fine,' I offered in a similar tone.

'Mmmhmm,' he said, almost to himself. There were a few seconds of awkward silence and I didn't have the energy to fill it. 'And . . . how is Veronica? Did you see her this morning?' he asked, trying to sound nonchalant.

It took a few seconds to register. '*Mum*, you mean?' I snapped, crossing my arms across my chest. I hated it when he went out of his way to be cold.

'Yes, her.' If his tone had been a food, it would have been a lemon, that's how bitter he sounded.

I wasn't sure how to answer so I decided to go with the truth. 'She's good, I think. Finding her way. She says she's going to start teaching yoga again.'

Out of all of us, losing Mike had hit Mum the hardest. Seeing her get a little bit of her strength and spark back had secretly made me feel as though maybe I had permission to be happy too. I hoped that Dad would see that Mum being happy again was a good thing, no matter what it meant for them.

'I see. Instead of focusing on keeping the family up and running, she's doing downward-facing dog,' he scoffed.

I felt my hands ball up into tight fists. 'You know what, Dad, no disrespect, but between running to work every chance you get and locking yourself in the study when you're home, what have *you* done to keep this family up and running?' I kept my gaze fixed on the road ahead, not at him, almost afraid of the truth that had finally been able to escape my throat.

Thankfully, we were at a red light. I had no doubt hearing me speak to him this way would have cost Dad his concentration. I risked a glance over at him.

'Excuse me! Have you—' he began, his grip on the steering wheel so tight his knuckles were white.

I interrupted him. 'I bet you're going to say I have no right to speak about your lack of support. Or about how it feels like it's just been Mum and me for the past two years? Like we've been a single-parent family, living with a lodger who likes to keep himself to himself.'

He slammed his hands on the steering wheel. While this would usually have scared me back into silence, today freedom overcame fear. I went on.

'Or maybe you're going to suggest that *we're* the problem? That you've done all you can, but we need to stop moping around, brush our sadness and grief under the carpet and just forget about it? That I need to listen to whatever you say, date a boy I don't even like, just so that I can make the right connections, go to the right university, live in the right area, so that I'll never end up in the same place Mike did?' I continued, unable to stop myself now, my throat burning with unshed tears.

The traffic light had turned green. He stepped on the accelerator with no caution and the car took off at sudden speed. 'You're just like your mother,' he growled. 'You have no respect. You don't value what I've done, all the sacrifices I've made. And my Lord in Heaven, if you were being raised back home, you would never speak to me this way. You would have been beaten from Sunday to Sunday. You – you British children have no respect, not for your parents and not for the law. This is why we are in this mess!' he yelled, his Nigerian accent now front and centre.

The same self-righteous rant. Every single time. 'You know what? Mike got lucky. At least he's free of you now,' I screamed back.

There was total silence. I clasped my hand over my mouth, wishing I could take the words back, knowing I had gone too far.

At that exact moment, the sound of his mobile ringing came through the car speakers. I looked at the screen and saw that it was the hospital. The high-pitched tone rang three times before I even dared to look his way. He wasn't answering it. He *never* ignored a phone call from work. 'It could be the difference between life and death,' he always warned, before answering no matter where we were.

I inched the top half of my body forward to get a better look at him and it was then I saw he was crying. I inhaled sharply, pressing myself back into my seat, willing it to open up and swallow me whole.

I had never, ever seen my dad cry.

Not when Mum called him in Germany to say the police had just been round.

Not when he made a speech at the funeral.

Not when he came home after the last day of the trial, when only one of Mike's murderers was found guilty of manslaughter.

Not even at the graveside, when the sound of the dirt hitting Mike's coffin was so loud in my ears I thought it could be heard in every corner of the world.

He hadn't shed a tear.

I didn't know what to do. I sat there paralysed as we finished the drive home in silence.

As we pulled into the drive, I opened the car door before he'd even put the handbrake on. Mum's car was already there, so I yanked the front door open, knowing it would be unlocked.

'Hi, love, how was your—' she began, but I ran right past her, up the stairs and into my room. I slammed the door and then I lunged on to my unmade bed, letting myself wail into my pillow. I allowed my lungs to open up and I screamed deep into the mattress. I kicked my legs as if I could swim away from this, but the only water to be found was the kind escaping my eyes. I cried for Mike, I cried for myself and I cried for what all of this had done to our family, for the way that his death had broken us into pieces, pieces that wouldn't fit back together again, no matter how much we tried.

I must have tired myself out from crying and fallen asleep, as when I came to, it was practically dark outside. The only light came from the hallway, through a crack in my bedroom door.

Slowly, I rolled over.

'AHHHHHHHHH!' I yelled. There was a figure sitting at the end of the bed.

'Aht aht, Cynthia, calm down now.' I was shocked to hear Dad's voice.

Instinctively, I sat up and drew my knees into my chest, trying to make myself as small as possible. I was awake enough to realise that, unlike Thomas at the sports shed, making Dad cry really had happened. He was probably here to tell me to pack so he could send me to Nigeria.

But when he spoke his voice wasn't angry. 'The fact that you recoil from me makes me sad. It shows how much I have changed.' He sighed, moving from the bed to my desk chair, as if to signify that this was a safe space. 'Do you mind?' he asked, indicating that he wanted to switch my desk lamp on.

I shrugged and he flicked the switch, momentarily blinding me with the sudden brightness. When my eyes adjusted to the light, I saw how old he looked, how tired, and it scared me.

'Listen, Dad, I'm sorry for what—' I started, nervous. His raised palm silenced me.

He took a deep breath. 'It is I who must apologise, Cynthia,' he said, not looking at me but towards the dark window, which showed him only his own reflection in return.

My head snapped up so suddenly I smacked my head on the wall behind me. 'Oww,' I whined quietly.

He chuckled. 'Forever our clumsy Cynthia,' he said with a small smile.

I frowned, rubbing the back of my head.

His gaze moved from the window to me, and he watched as I massaged the sore spot for a moment. 'When something hurts – whether it's physical like a bump on the head, or something less tangible, something . . . inside your head – it doesn't mean you should ignore it. In fact, completely the opposite. I tell my patients this all the time.'

I stayed silent, waiting for him to make his point.

'But I have been ignoring my own advice, trying to run away from the pain, instead of facing it head on. What you said in the car, it hurt me nearly as much as losing my son.' His tone dipped towards the end of the sentence. 'But, like the pain of losing him, what you said cannot be ignored. Everything you said was true.' His voice cracked. It was clearly painful for him to come to this realisation.

I shuffled forward on the bed, feeling safe enough to begin to close the gap between us.

'I am not like you,' he said, his tone formal still. 'You, your mother . . . you are open and sensitive. Your brother was like this too. You share what you're feeling at any given moment. I – I wasn't raised that way. The space allotted for me to say how I feel died when your grandparents did. I had to become a man and raise my siblings. Any sign of weakness would have ruined us. I need you to understand that. I need you to understand where I'm coming from.' He looked at me with a searching gaze.

I nodded my head slowly. I did understand.

'Parents are supposed to know how to handle everything,' he said, standing up and walking over to my window. 'But I haven't known how to handle this. I know I have always been hard on you, but it's because I wanted the world for you. You and your brother. And once Mike died, that is when I knew that as hard as I tried, I could never fully protect you. And instead of telling you that I was scared, I withdrew. I tried to control everything even more. Now you are all suffering because of it. And for that I'm sorry.' He came to sit next to me on the bed. 'I am truly sorry,' he said again, his voice breaking.

In one swift move, I threw my arms around his neck and we sat there as we cried silently. As I hugged him, I realised the last time I had been this close to him was the weekend before that day.

We were gathered around the kitchen table, about to start a game of Monopoly. For as long as I could remember, we'd played Monopoly in pairs. Dad and I on one team, playing with our heads. Mum and Mike on the other, playing with their hearts. Mum had suggested we switch things up this game.

'Let me stay with my baby girl,' Dad said, pulling me in for a hug. 'I like winning. And you two always end up flat broke within half an hour,' he added, jutting his chin towards Mum and Mike.

'We can't all be heartless capitalists!' Mum shot back with a wink, reaching for her trusty thimble piece, a sign of how old the board we played was.

'Exactly!' Mike said. 'Some of us were born to change the world for the better.'

'I have no doubt you will do that,' Dad said. 'Both of you,' he added, gently squeezing my shoulder. I let myself relax into his arms and he gave me a kiss on the top of the head.

'Now, let's get 'em, Cyn,' he said with a laugh, and the rest of us joined in.

Tonight, in a world that felt far, far away from that one, we sat together in comfortable silence, until I heard Mum shout that dinner was almost ready.

'What about . . . Mum?' I asked as he began to stand up, wanting to know if the divorce was still happening, wanting to know if he was going to apologise to her too, but scared to ask.

'She's put up with a lot from me, Cynthia.' He stretched to his full height. 'It sometimes feels as though I'm cursed. Even though I am a surgeon it feels as though nothing that I love can survive.' His words hit my stomach like cement blocks.

'But I won't let our love perish without a fight,' he finished. With a kiss on the top of my head, he slipped out of my bedroom door, leaving me alone to process all that just happened.

CHAPTER EIGHTEEN

The next morning, I woke up before my alarm, feeling content. At dinner the previous night, Dad had made a real effort with both me and Mum. I wasn't sure what he'd said to her while I'd been in my room, but if I'd had to guess I would have said they'd put a pause on the divorce conversation, at least for now. Mum was still guarded, but if Dad really wanted to save our family, I was sure there was a chance he'd succeed. Which was enough for me. That night I'd slept as soundly as I had before everything had changed for ever. Maybe we *could* get through this.

Things were looking up. I was starting to feel settled at Thornton's. I now felt comfortable enough in my long-distance friendship with Jadell to know that neither of us could ever replace the other. And, of course, there was Isaac. My face broke into a smile just thinking about him.

I pulled my phone so it released itself from the charger to check how early it was. My hair had started to return to its tight coils and I would have to be mindful about how much time I'd need to wrestle it into a bun.

Waiting for me was a text from Isaac. My smile quickly faded as I read it.

> **Not feeling well**
> **Wont be in today**
> **XXX**

My heart sank a little. I was looking forward to seeing him.

> **Awww man**
> **See you tomorrow?**
> **X**

I threw the phone on to the bed and began to get ready.

About half an hour later, I came down the stairs to find that Dad was still home. This was unusual, so I approached the kitchen with caution. Peeking around the corner, I relaxed a little.

Mum and Dad were both sitting on bar stools at the island. Mum was typing furiously on her laptop and Dad was peering over his glasses and scrolling through his phone. They weren't talking, but they were sitting so close together that should either of them move, the other would feel it.

I coughed theatrically to alert them of my presence.

'Morning, honey!' Mum beamed.

I waved sheepishly.

'I didn't do a full spread today. But there's scrambled egg, spicy baked beans and some bacon in the microwave. You're going to have to fix your toast yourself.' She waved her hand in the direction of the toaster.

I giggled. That was Mum, always going above and beyond and then acting like it was nothing.

'Sleep well?' Dad asked, looking up from his phone.

'Mmmhmm. Best sleep I've had in ages,' I admitted, punching the buttons on the microwave. 'Dad, can you drive me to school on your way to work today?' I asked.

'I've decided to take the morning off work,' Dad said.

I looked at him in shock, then at Mum. She winked at me. 'Do you think he's sick, Cyn?' she asked me, using her palm to feel his forehead, as if she were checking his temperature.

He laughed and shook his head. 'It's a sad state of affairs when your family thinks you're unwell because you are taking some much-needed time off. But –' he continued, putting his phone down entirely and smacking his hands together – 'perhaps in a way, you're right. I haven't been my usual self. I am going to try and get better, for all of us.'

Mum squeezed his shoulder, smiling gently. *Maybe this was going to work out*, I thought to myself as I took my breakfast out of the microwave.

'I can drop you off today,' Mum told me.

'I miss just being able to take the number two,' I sighed. 'No offence,' I added hastily.

'None taken!' Mum shot back. 'You know, yesterday I had to drive forty-five minutes for plantain. I was furious.' She sighed.

'I must admit, it's taking me longer than expected to find my feet at this hospital. It's like I'm having to prove myself all over again,' Dad said.

It felt good for us all to be on the same page. This was a massive life change. It was OK to acknowledge that.

'But do these teething issues mean we should return to London?' Dad asked.

'No,' we all said in unison. Though I was sure my reasons were different to my parents'. The image of Isaac's face flashed into my mind.

'Well, at least we all agree on something,' said Mum.

Forty-five minutes later, I slid into the passenger seat next to Mum. I waited until we were a few minutes away from the house before I began my interrogation.

'So . . . Dad came into my room last night and basically showed me all the emotions,' I said.

'Same with me,' she admitted with a soft sigh.

There were a few moments of silence.

'And?' I prompted. 'What does that mean? Are you still going to get a divorce?'

She shot me one of her *I'm not one of your little friends* looks.

'Sorry,' I said hastily. 'But, Mum, throw me a bone here! I'm just trying to know if we're heading back to where we can get plantain and X-Pressions on every street corner.'

'Girl, you really are my child,' she chuckled, reaching over to squeeze my chin. She let out a big sigh before speaking again. 'Cyn, relationships are hard. And your dad closing down when I most needed him to open up has hurt me in a way that is going to take us some time to recover from.'

I nodded my head slowly.

'Your dad says he is committed to doing what needs to be done, not only to save this marriage but, more importantly, himself. I said I can give him time to do that. But I'm going to need more elbow grease and less flapping lips.'

I relaxed a little. At least she was willing to give him another chance. That was all I could have asked for.

'You're growing up, Cyn. If there is one thing I want you to keep in mind, it's that a man – or a boy, in your case – will always show you who he really is. Words are cheap, but actions reveal the truth. If he is a good person, if he really cares about you, you will know. You will feel it. So many people questioned why I would marry your father. We were from such different backgrounds. But listen, I knew he was a decent person, and I knew that he loved me. He said it, but he also proved it with his actions every single day. Over the last couple of years, we've lost our way. But I have never doubted that he is a good man. And that is the most important thing. Always go with the good boy, the one who treats you like you matter. Because you do. OK?' she finished sternly.

'OK,' I said lightly.

'I mean it, Cynthia,' she pressed.

'OK! OK!' I cried, slightly embarrassed. But it felt as though now was as good a time as ever to tell her about Isaac. 'Speaking of boys,' I began. 'I have . . . a date with one. This weekend. If I'm allowed,' I added quickly, realising I hadn't exactly asked permission.

'Oooooh, my baby girl is growing up!' she cooed, reaching over to squeeze my chin again.

I swatted her hand away.

'Is this the boy that we went against your daddy for?' she asked.

'Uhhh, yeah. Yeah, it is,' I said.

'Well then, I already support your union. Let me know when I need to buy a hat,' she cackled.

'Mum!' I moaned. I quickly glanced at the time. We were at least ten minutes away from school still. 'The thing is though – his brother likes me too. That's the boy Dad wanted me to choose. And I feel like it's going to cause aggro,' I said, glad to finally be able to voice my worry aloud.

'For who?' Mum snapped. 'Not my baby girl, cos I will be ready to—'

'Mum, no violence necessary.' I laughed, throwing my hands up. 'I just think it's going to cause bad vibes between the two of them,' I said, turning to look out of the window.

'Listen, Cyn,' said Mum, serious now. 'This is a story as old as time, two friends, or in this case, brothers—'

'*Adopted* brothers,' I interrupted.

'Adopted brothers are still brothers, Cyn. You don't have to share blood to be a family. Anyway, so two brothers both like the same girl. In prehistoric times they probably would have clubbed each other to see who would win you. I'm sure your own brother would have known the details,' she added with a small smile. 'In the Middle Ages, I guess they would have duelled it out with swords. Thankfully, times have changed, and you can make your own decision, *and* no one needs to learn how to fight. If they have a true brotherly bond, *you* following your heart shouldn't diminish the love *they* have for each other,' she concluded, slapping the steering wheel as if to punctuate the sentence.

'You're right.' I shrugged, feeling a little lighter. *Not that there seems to be much brotherly love between them though*, I thought.

'You know what, Cyn . . . I think I am!' she guffawed.

We spent the rest of the drive singing along to the only radio station in this area that ever played R&B – it was pretty much the same two tracks on a loop throughout the day, but it was something – and I arrived at school sure that everything would sort itself out. So sure, in fact, that even when I clocked that Thomas was lingering near the entrance of the school, I waved Mum off, feeling one hundred per cent confident about telling him the truth and believing that he would be mature enough to understand.

But as he approached me, the scowl on his face immediately knocked that one hundred down to ten.

'Hi—' I started.

'You should have just told me, Cynthia,' he interrupted.

'Hiiiii, Thomas, nice to see you too,' I tried again, keeping my voice even, although my heart had now doubled in pace.

'I saw you!' he whisper-hissed, clearly not wanting to draw too much attention to our conversation. I could sense that all ears around us were already cocked in our direction.

'This morning? I have quite literally just walked in, so unless there's a new Black girl I don't know about, then I'm pretty sure you haven't seen anyone that looks like me today,' I said lightly, deliberately misunderstanding him and trying to step around him to get to the door.

He swiftly blocked me, bringing me to a sudden stop.

'Where you're from it may be cool to play dumb, Cynthia. but around here we take intelligence and honesty very seriously,' he huffed, sounding more like a chastising teacher than ever. 'You disappoint me.'

My eyes grew wide with anger. 'Who the fuck do you think you're chatting to?' I spat, shedding my fake Home Counties demeanour and stepping into my true, grittier south London self. 'Listen, I'm not one of them eediyat bwoys on the rugby team who thinks you're God, and I'm not one of the teachers who has to kiss your pale ass just so they can keep their job,' I growled, and kissed my teeth. I was now so close to him, I was sure he could taste what I had for breakfast. 'You want to talk? Let's talk. Yes, I lied to you. And you know what, I felt bad about it. But I was trying to let you down gently. And you wouldn't take no for an answer, would you? You kept trying your luck, even when I told you I couldn't date you. And the thing was, you had been so kind, and I didn't want to hurt you. But if you had just listened to me, we wouldn't be in this situation. And now I don't give a shit, bruv. So you want the truth? Yes, I am interested in someone else. And yes, you did see me kissing your brother.'

I heard a few sharp intakes of breath around me.

'What. The. Fuck. About. It. Huh?' I finished.

He took a step back and I thought I saw a flash of fear dance across his eyes.

'Miss AH-DAY-GO-KAY! What on earth is going on here?' It was Mrs Marshall. I bet one of these do-goody kids had alerted her. How annoying. At St Martin's a teacher wouldn't even care until the first punch had been thrown. Sometimes even the second.

I kissed my teeth again. There were a few seconds of awkward silence.

'Explain yourself!' she demanded, looking only at me.

I was flabbergasted. Had I been arguing with *myself*? I opened my mouth to let rip, but Thomas interrupted me.

'It's me who needs to explain,' he said, facing Mrs Marshall. 'I disagreed with something Cynthia said and I wasn't very polite about it. She was just . . . uh, setting me right,' he added, nodding towards me.

Man, this boy could act. I rolled my eyes.

'Well . . . as long as everything is under control,' Mrs Marshall huffed finally, looking between us.

'I can assure you it is,' I snapped, trying to claw back some respect.

'Very well. The bell will go soon. Hurry off to class, all of you,' she said, addressing the crowd that had gathered around us, and then going back inside.

Without another glance at Thomas, I followed the other students to the door, heading towards my form room.

'Cyn . . . thia, wait up!' Thomas called, jogging to catch up with me. He grabbed my elbow.

I shoved it straight into his side. 'Don't you ever, *ever* lay a hand on me. Next time, you'll get it back with three fingers,' I snarled.

'Ouch,' he said, rubbing his ribs. 'OK, I got it. But hey, please listen. I'm sorry about just now.'

'Really? You're *sorry*? Do you know how hard it is for me to be here? To be practically one of one? If it's not Barbie bitches making fun of my hair, it's a moment like that, where I'm singled out as the *only* one making trouble. I don't need to be blacklisted, Thomas! I'm Black enough!' I started to walk again.

'Listen. Wait!' he begged once more.

I stopped so suddenly that he crashed into me. I turned on my heel. His hands were up as if in surrender and his face looked truly distraught. For the first time, when I looked at him, I didn't see a handsome, privileged young man but just a boy, my age, who had made a mess of things. That, I could understand.

'I am truly sorry, Cynthia. I screwed up. I was . . . I was jealous. I admit it,' he said ruefully. 'I went about everything the wrong way from the very beginning. I see that now. But . . . the thing is, Isaac isn't telling you everything, Cynthia. You don't know who he really is.'

I sighed loudly. So much for his apology. It had just been another attempt to try and sabotage me and Isaac.

'You sound crazy,' I snapped, tapping my temple twice. 'Do you need my dad to refer you to someone, or can you pay privately?'

'Very funny,' he responded with a straight face. 'Cynthia, I mean it. This isn't going to end well.'

'Only if you make it difficult for us!' I spat out angrily.

'That . . . that's not entirely true,' he said, clearly exasperated.

'Listen, Thomas, I apologise for not being straight with you. But I like Isaac. I really do. And nothing you do or say is going to change that, OK?' I shrugged, no longer caring who might overhear me. Yet again I saw it, that same flash of rage momentarily crossing his face.

He took a step back from me, his hands up again, this time as if to prove he meant no harm. I turned on my heel and began

163

to stride towards class, but then I heard him mutter under his breath, 'We'll see about that.'

By the time I turned around to dare him to say it again, he was gone.

CHAPTER NINETEEN

I was secretly thankful when Isaac told me he wasn't going to be in for the rest of the week due to a tummy bug. I didn't think I had the energy to deal with Thomas and his awkward behaviour in front of Isaac just yet. And then there was the whole 'We'll see about that' line, which had made me feel uneasy. Where I was from, that would have been a threat, so now I felt as though I had to watch my back, on top of everything else. It was a lot to contend with. I hoped that by the time Isaac returned to school next week it would all have burnt off and things could go back to (relative) normality.

The week zipped by in a flurry of lessons and family dinners with Mum and Dad, which were actually quite nice. Dad was trying really hard to integrate himself back into the family fold and prove himself to Mum. But there was one big roadblock: Mum was still struggling to get him to agree to attend counselling with her.

'I just don't understand your father's aversion to it,' she complained, checking the mirrors before sharply swerving into the overtaking lane.

It was five o'clock on Friday evening and we had made the unwise decision to travel into London. It seemed like everyone who lived outside of the M25 had had the same idea.

However, as Isaac had texted me that morning to assure me that our date tomorrow was still on, I was more than willing to put up with rush-hour traffic if it meant being able to get my hair done.

With the damp weather we'd had the last few days, my blowout had – quite literally – recoiled, and once again my hair was an afro that was putting tension on both my arms and hair tools. After trying and failing to locate a Black hairstylist nearby who didn't charge a premium because of their posh postcode, Mum and I agreed that looking pretty was worth heading to London. Of course, I was taking this as an opportunity to link up with Jadell too. She'd said she would pick up my X-Pressions and then swing by Auntie June's after meeting someone. *Someone* meant a boy, of course. But for once I was too preoccupied with my own love life to investigate who it was. In any case, I loved J, but I knew there would be another one in a month or so. She didn't have the patience for anything serious. But I rated J's commitment to no commitment hard, because where other girls had fallen under the 'promiscuous/hoe/sket/slag' categories just for being seen with two boys in the same year, J wore her sexuality with pride.

'Listen, ain't no boy finna try hold me down and I don't know if he has the right key for this lock!' she once joked.

I admired that about her. Although the combination of pretty privilege and popularity meant that even if other girls *thought* she was a sket, no one would have dared say it to her face.

It's like she knew I was thinking about her, because at that

166

exact moment my phone began to ring, interrupting Mum's rant about Dad.

'Girl, what hair do you need again? 1B, innit? Not 1?' she yelled, as soon as I answered. The background noises made me guess she was at the market.

'Uh, yeah, 1B. I think jet black would be a bit harsh,' I replied.

'You should try it,' Mum interjected. 'It would really make your eyes stand out.'

'Yeah, Mumsy is right, you know – HELLO, MUM – 1B is so *safe*,' she said.

'Hi, J!' Mum yelled back.

'Oh my word, do you two want to talk to each other?' I laughed. 'Honestly, 1B is great and I should only need two packs – maybe three to be on the safe side. I don't want Auntie June cussing.'

'OK. Bossman, can I get three 1Bs? . . . Yeah, the X Pressions . . . SINCE WHEN WAS IT FOUR POUNDS? AM I A MUG . . . ?!' J yelled, before the line went dead.

Mum and I laughed.

'One day that girl is gonna give herself a heart attack,' Mum said, shaking her head.

'Innit,' I agreed, cracking up.

'Anyway, back to Dad,' I said, remembering what we'd been discussing before the call. 'Mum, you know how – no offence – your generation are about therapy. It just wasn't a *thing* back then. It's gonna take him some time to come around to the idea. Please bear with him,' I begged. 'It seems like he's actually really trying.'

167

She kissed her teeth but didn't argue, which was a win for me. Admittedly, I wanted their marriage to work for my own reasons too. A few months ago, it might have been a blessing for them to spend some time apart. Two weeks ago, I would have been thrilled for Mum and me to head back to London. But now . . . there was Isaac. I didn't want to go through picking up and moving my life again, and I knew that if Mum and Dad couldn't make it work, Mum would more than likely move back to London, and I'd go with her. Not only was that where her support network was, it's where Big Mike was too. The day we'd had to decide what to do with Mike's body was still burned into my memory.

'A burial is a lot more expensive,' said Dad.

'We are not going to talk about fucking expense as my son lays frozen in a morgue – do you understand me, Babatunde?' Mum growled.

None of us had slept properly in weeks. It was one hour here and an hour there, whenever our bodies finally succumbed to the exhaustion. The doorbell went so often during those first few days that I'd stopped noticing it. At one point I found myself wondering if there were any more flowers left in the entire world, given how many we'd received.

And the food. Jollof, jerk chicken, rice and peas, plantain and dumplings. We could have fed the entire neighbourhood and still had plenty left over. But Mum, Dad and I couldn't eat anything. As fast as it arrived, Mum made calls to have other families come and collect it. Whatever was left after that she stored in the chest freezer in the garage. The never-ending checklist of admin that had come with the death kept us all too busy to clock the zombies we were turning into.

'If only we knew what he wanted,' Dad said sadly.

'Well, we kind of do,' I croaked. 'I mean, I do.'

The look in the two sets of bloodshot eyes encouraged me to keep talking.

'When Uncle Norman died and we went to that place where they toasted him—'

'The crematorium, where they cremated him,' Dad corrected, sounding strained.

'Umm, yeah, that. Mike leaned over to me and was like, "If I go first and they put me in fire before I've even had the chance to see if I can talk my way out of hell, I'll kill you".' I couldn't help but smile at the memory.

There was a long silence and then Mum began to laugh. 'Michael!' she called out between chuckles. 'Oh, Michael!' she cried again, clutching her chest. Then . . . 'MICHAEL!' she screamed, her laughs turning to sobs.

Dad slid off the bar stool and tried to hug her, even as she started to hit him in the chest. He fended off blow after blow, until she had exhausted herself.

I silently wiped my own tears away.

'You give my baby boy whatever he wants,' she whimpered. 'Whatever he wants,' she repeated, exhausted.

'OK,' said Dad.

And because we didn't yet realise how hard it would be to keep living in a house where three were once four, we buried Mike in the cemetery of the church where we had sporadically attended Sunday school, the same one that was connected to my secondary school. There

169

was something comforting about being able to pop in on him every day, to know that I could just look out of one of the back windows at school and see his headstone.

It was only much later, when it became clear that Dad was not willing to compromise on leaving London, that the limitations of our decision became clear.

'But what about Mike?' Mum sobbed.

'Veronica, you exhaust me. Mike is gone. What remains is exactly that, his remains. The cost and legality surrounding an exhumation is not worth it. You can come and visit whenever you like,' he said.

'Of course, it will only be me visiting him,' she spat back.

He didn't answer.

My vibrating phone pulled me back to the present day. Mum had been right about her being the only one going back to visit Mike's grave. I hadn't been able to face it yet, in the weeks since we'd moved, and I knew Dad hadn't been for months. Even when we were still living in London he'd avoided it. Today Mum was planning to drop me off at the hairdresser's and then head to the cemetery just to check on him. I didn't mind. It gave me more time to catch up with J. My phone buzzed again. It was Isaac.

> Can't w8 for 2morrow
> Missed you this week
> X

My face broke into a wide smile.

'Mmmhmm, I remember being your age and smiling like that,' Mum said, chuckling. 'Is he cute?'

'Urghhh, Mummmmm,' I said, feeling myself blush.

'Hey, I was young once, you know. I'm old but I'm—'

'Not cold!' I finished for her, laughing.

'That's right,' she said with a click of her fingers, before turning up the radio and singing along.

I was about to put my phone back in my bag when I suddenly remembered the email that Thomas said he'd sent me last weekend. I sighed but thought I'd better check, in case it was something important. I just hoped it wasn't another plea for a date, or perhaps a further offer to help me with my maths.

Logging in to my school account, I quickly scrolled past a load of boring notices about sports fixtures, GCSE revision sessions and charity bake sales until I found Thomas's email.

He'd reached out to me in his capacity as editor of the school newspaper to ask if I'd contribute an article for the next issue about my experiences moving from the impoverished slums of south London to the refined and rarefied Buckinghamshire countryside. He didn't quite put it like that, of course, but not far off.

I rolled my eyes, chucked my phone in my bag and hummed along with Mum to Mary J. Blige as we sped along, all the while daydreaming about tomorrow and my date with Isaac.

CHAPTER TWENTY

It took another hour to get to Auntie June's salon. Mum found a parking spot right outside. As ever, we couldn't see through the windows because the steam from the multiple overhead dryers, tongs and straighteners created condensation that acted like blinds. When we were younger, Big Mike and I would write backwards on the glass so people could read our cheeky messages from the outside. With so much of the surrounding area changing, it was a relief to know Auntie June's was still here.

'It feels good to be home,' Mum announced as she got out of the car, stretching.

I took a deep inhale, nodding in agreement before stepping into the salon.

'Girrrrl!' J squealed, leaping out of her chair so quickly she sent magazines flying.

'Listen, Cyn, talk ti yuh likkle fren!' Auntie June laughed. 'Mi nah want the shop buss down cah she cyan't control she h'excitement.'

'Sorry, Auntie June,' huffed J. 'But this is my best friend!' Squealing, she threw herself at me, and we hugged and jumped up and down together.

'Lord, people wouldn't believe that they spend every evening either on the phone or texting one another, you know,' Mum laughed. 'Listen, June, where yuh wan mi fi put dese tings?' she asked. It had been a while since I had heard her speak patois and it made me smile.

The box of things was for Auntie June's son, who was the age Mike would have been if we hadn't lost him. Mum had slowly started to go through his belongings and give away the bits that weren't of sentimental value. When I'd seen her put a box of his stuff in the car to bring to Auntie June, I wanted to stop her. To drag the box back to what should have been Mike's room. But I didn't want to interrupt her healing process. We were all going to manage this differently and I had to accept that.

'Oh! Bring dem come – them is not just any tings. Luke will be so grateful. *I* am grateful,' she exclaimed, coming towards Mum. She looked at her softly and they silently embraced. Perhaps exchanging an energy that only mothers who were without their sons understood. They silently rocked back and forth.

Auntie June wasn't actually related to us, but she had been family for ever. When Mum was pregnant with Mike, her water broke in Auntie June's salon. As kids, when Mum couldn't find a sitter or Dad was running late, we'd make our way to the shop. Mike and I would play with her kids, Luke and Chloe – only stopping to eat either McDonald's or rice, peas and jerk chicken – until we passed out or someone came to retrieve us, whichever came first.

But now, Mike was dead and Luke was in prison. Luke had got caught up in the other side of it all, easily groomed into joining a gang when Auntie June was just busy trying to keep him in a good school and keep the salon afloat. Raising Black boys in south London was no joke. We used to hear the older folk say, 'You'll end up in one of two places, either dead or in prison.' I'd never taken it seriously until it started to happen around me and I experienced first-hand what it did to families, to our communities. Mum and Auntie June had both lost their sons, in different ways, and in the absence of anyone else who understood, they had to console each other through the harsh realities of these streets. But unlike Mike, Luke wasn't gone for ever. He was due out soon, which is why Mum had brought some of Mike's things for him.

Auntie June and Mum finally released each other.

'Listen, I'm just gonna run and see Mike really quick,' Mum said, wiping her eyes.

'Yes, tell him I said hi and we miss him,' Auntie June replied, before turning to me. 'Now, Miss Cyn, what am I doing for you today? Dem countryside stylists can't make style buss like we, right?' she cackled.

'Yes, Auntie, you're right about that,' J cut in, giggling.

I playfully swatted her with my backpack. 'I was thinking straight back canerows, bum-grazing. Simple but still fly,' I said, looking at my currently not-so-fly self in the mirror.

'Understood,' said Auntie June. 'You got the hair?'

'Check!' said J, holding the bag of X-Pressions aloft as if we were about to start major surgery.

'Good girls,' she praised. 'Let me just finish up with this client and we'll get to work.' She rushed back to the woman she'd been with, who looked like she was about to faint from the heat of the overhead dryer.

174

J made sure Auntie June was fully engaged with her client before turning to me with a wicked grin. 'Bitch, I want to know EVERYTHING!' she shrieked.

I put the back of my hand to my forehead and played like I was about to faint. 'Jayyyyyyy,' I squealed. 'Why is this boy so fine, please?'

'Uhhh, because the countryside don't have no pollution!' she mocked, rolling her eyes.

I slapped her knee. 'Nah, seriously, he just . . . gets it. Gets *me*, I guess. Like when my hair was straightened, he said it was nice but that he preferred it like this, cos it reminded him of home.' I tugged at my hair to illustrate my point.

'OK! Man's got bars! Stop it because I'm feeling things!' she joked, pretending to fan herself.

I grimaced, screwing up my face. She spotted my expression and shoved my arm lightly. 'You won't be playing prim and proper for ever, babes, trust me on that.'

I shuddered. Kissing was one thing but beyond that? No, I wasn't thinking about anything more just yet. I wasn't ready. But I had to admit the idea of *one day* doing more with Isaac did make my heart beat a little faster . . .

'Cyn! Cum here mek we start di ting so yuh muddah ain't driving home at the crack of dawn,' Auntie June called, brandishing a towel.

Me and J headed to the back of the salon where the sinks were.

'Damn, yuh hair still tick and niceeee,' Auntie June complimented as she freed my hair from my scrunchie. 'Come mek me wash it and you can tell me all about dis bwoy.'

Who told her? I shot J a look, but she shrugged.

'Hmph, yuh tink sey I was born yesterday?' Auntie June asked. 'All dem tricks I played them,' she added, as if she had read my mind.

I giggled.

'Plus, yah muddah already told me,' she cackled.

'Arggghhh, Mum!' I groaned, as I settled into the nook in the sink.

'Listen, Cynthia, you're all she has, OK?' Auntie June reminded me, dropping her patois and seamlessly flowing into south London twang. 'She just wants the best for you. Watching you grow up is hard. It's the same for me with Chloe. We know the madness that awaits you all. Even you, J. You girls are all we have,' she said again. 'So don't mind if we talk about you. It's cos we love all of you, OK?' She looked down on me from above.

I nodded so I wouldn't have to speak. Because I knew if I did, I would cry. I'd missed this. This sisterhood. This community. This sense of belonging. Sure, our house was bigger and the air was fresher, but nothing could replace the hustle and bustle of the city, how easy it was to pick up plantain and yam on the way home and the feeling of not being the only one of anything.

For the rest of the evening, I just allowed myself to enjoy the things that I'd missed. The music, the laughter, the gossip, all of it. What a barbershop was to Black men, what the pub was to white people – that was what a place like Auntie June's was to Black women. It was the meeting spot. A place to get advice, catch jokes and even, if necessary, get reprimanded. I hadn't realised how much I'd missed it until now.

176

When Mum returned, she seemed rejuvenated.

'How is our boy?' Auntie June asked.

'Fine. A little in need of some upkeep but nothing I couldn't manage,' Mum answered with a smile.

Even with Auntie June starting on me early, it was just before midnight by the time we were done and helping her close up. Not that any of us were complaining. We had ordered some West Indian takeaway around seven and spent the next five hours putting the world to rights. The evening had passed by in a blur. And one thing was for certain, my hair looked fire. Auntie June's hands were truly blessed. Every canerow was the same size and the partings were sharp and precise. She'd artfully steered my baby hairs into the prettiest squiggles.

'Now, for the love of God, Cyn-tia, nuh buddah forget yuh head tie tonight! Yuh nuh yuh wan fil look fresh and nice fi tomorrow,' she ordered.

I walked over to my backpack and pulled out my silk headscarf as if I were performing a magic trick, waving it around before beginning to tie it down.

'Good gurl!' Auntie June exclaimed. 'V! Mek sure you give her one nice earring, sumting vibey, mek her beauty show.'

'Yes, June, nuh worry bout dat,' Mum shot back.

Once the shop was secure, we all said our goodbyes and me and J jumped into Mum's car so we could give her a ride home. We were both so tired that we drove in silence, J's head resting on my shoulder and my heart feeling full. I'd missed this so much. The drive to J's wasn't a long one, but we both fell asleep and Mum had to nudge us awake. J and I said our sleepy goodbyes in the car, while our mums caught up on the doorstep.

'Babe, video-call me when you're picking an outfit tomorrow, I beg,' J whispered as she got out of the car.

'Girl, of course,' I replied sleepily, stepping out and pulling her in for one last hug. I felt oddly emotional – in the groggy, half-awake kind of way you do after a long night with loved ones – as I watched J give Mum a quick hug before heading inside.

My phone pinged just as Mum got back into the car. It was from Isaac.

All of a sudden, I was wide awake.

Can't wait 2 see u XX

I spent the rest of the drive back home with a smile on my face.

CHAPTER TWENTY-ONE

The next morning, the first thing I did when I woke up was to touch my head. Thankfully my headscarf was still securely on.

I swung my legs off the bed and sat on the edge for a minute

'It's a big day today,' I said to myself, reaching to snatch my phone off the charger.

There was already a text message from Isaac.

> Hope u slept well
> I'll pick you up later, what's ur address?
> XXX

The XXXs gave me instant butterflies, but I was thrown by him asking to pick me up. How? He didn't have a driving licence. And if he came by the house, he would have to come in and meet Mum and Dad. I knew I wouldn't get away with anything less. Arghhhh. This was *not* how it was supposed to go. But I shrugged my shoulders and decided to play it cool.

> Sleep was GR8
> Sure u can pick me up

Im at 18 hubbard road HP24 8RH

x

It felt like I barely had a chance to hit send before I had a reply.

I will be there at 6
XXX

I clocked that he still sent three Xs even though I'd only sent one and that made me like him even more. Even though J had always encouraged me to play hard to get, it felt like I didn't have to with Isaac. But now he was coming to get me, which wasn't part of the plan. I checked the time.

It was already 10.40 a.m. Even though logic said I had more than enough time to get ready, I still felt panicked. J wouldn't be back from kickboxing until at least midday and I wanted to be ready early just to avoid feeling rushed and then potentially sweating.

'Take a deep breath, Cyn,' I whispered to myself. *One thing at a time*, I thought. *First thing is food*.

As I opened my bedroom door, the strong smell of Saturday Soup hit my nose. I couldn't remember when Mum had last cooked this. Definitely not since we moved, as Dad hadn't been around, and it was mainly his favourite. Plus getting hold of the produce up here was hard. Last night, on her way back to the salon after visiting Mike, she'd stopped at the market and picked up all the staples: yam, green banana, Scotch bonnet,

180

pumpkin and, of course, the cock soup mix, which was something I still couldn't ask for without giggling.

I didn't have to get to the bottom of the stairs to confirm that Dad was home, as his voice drifted up to me. There was a new tone to his voice these days, and it made me feel warm and secure instead of filled with dread. He was in his study, on the phone, and the door was wide open. I didn't know if it was a peace offering or an invitation, but it made me smile nonetheless as I walked past and gave him a wave on my way to the kitchen.

As I came in, Mum was singing along to that old Sean Paul song 'I'm Still in Love with You', rocking back and forth in front of the hob and using a wooden spoon as a pretend microphone.

I playfully threw my hands over my ears.

'Oh, please, honey, you know I could've been the next big thing!' she laughed.

She wasn't lying. Her voice was incredible. But Mum, just like Dad, had shouldered a lot of responsibility early on in life, putting her dreams on the back burner to help her family through some rough times. Mum was whippet smart but, being from a tough part of south London, she wasn't encouraged to dream big, she was encouraged to get by – and to use whatever she earned to help support those around her. She would often say that it was the double curse of being the firstborn and a female. A girl didn't get to live her own life or have her own dreams. She had to be ready to support others. When she met Dad, he encouraged her to think bigger and to envision a life where she wasn't solely parenting children who weren't even hers. When they finally got married, most of the family said she had gotten 'rich and switched' – forgotten all about them. But she always told us that she finally felt free. The saddest thing was, she wasn't close to her family any more. She had made it out and her siblings had become spiteful and jealous. She always told me she never wanted feelings like that between me and Mike.

I signalled for Mum to turn the music down. I wanted to speak with her about tonight, before Dad could stick his nose in.

'So, Isaac offered to pick me up tonight . . .' I said slowly, taking a seat at the island.

'As he should,' she said firmly, walking over to the fridge.

'Really?' I asked with a screwed-up face.

'This is your first proper date. He asked you out. How else did he expect you to get there? Fly?' she enquired with a smile.

'Oh.' I was a little surprised by her assurance. 'But when Jadell goes on dates she just meets—' I was cut short by Mum holding her hand aloft.

'My sweet Cynthia.' She sighed. 'Listen, you know I love J like I love your cousins – more than some of them, in fact,' she added wickedly, 'but the boys she sees are not the kind of boys I want *you* to start dating. The reality is, those little hoodlums J is running around with only want one thing.'

My eyes grew wide.

'Don't play coy, Cynthia. Now isn't the time,' Mum said, suddenly sounding serious. 'The streets that raised J will already be calling her fast, loose or too grown. It's not her fault,' she added, seeing my face and forestalling my objection, 'and it's not fair that the judgement falls on her alone and not the boys, but that's the world we live in.' She gave a little hum of anger. 'But Jadell has never had proper guidance. And in the absence of true confidence in herself, she's getting her validation from boys. Any boy or man that comes before her, she will let them have a go. But everything that glitters ain't gold. Especially where we're from.' She sighed, before beginning to chop more carrots to throw into the pot.

I felt like I'd been punched in the gut. It must have shown on my face.

'Oh, sweetie. I know she's your friend, but her mum has let her own trauma get in the way of giving her the direction she needs. I don't want the same for you.' She looked at me with a piercing gaze.

I nodded my head.

'So yes, Isaac has the right idea,' she said, her tone becoming lighter. 'He'll pick you up, and he'll come in and meet us before you go on your date.' I groaned inwardly, but when she looked over at me, I nodded again.

'You got your GVM?' she asked abruptly, as if she'd just remembered.

'Uh well, I didn't think—'

'Nope! No thinking necessary, Cynthia. The point of Get Vex Money is so you can get yourself out of any situation, OK? If you're out of your allowance, just say.'

'OK, *OK*, Mum. And yeah . . . I may need a little top-up.' I cringed.

'I thought as much. Pass me my bag,' she ordered, using her

chin to point in the direction of her handbag, which was on the table in the conservatory.

I hopped off the bar stool to retrieve it.

'There should be a fifty-pound note in there. Take it, but don't spend it unless you have to. And bring me back my—'

'Change,' I said, finishing her sentence and slipping the money into the pocket of my PJs. I returned to my seat. The soup smelled so good. I inhaled deeply.

'You nervous?' She smiled, scooping the sliced carrots into the pot.

'Yeah,' I sighed.

'So is he,' she said.

'You think?' I asked.

'Of course. Especially since you chose him and not his brother,' she said. '*Adopted* brother, I know,' she said, rightly anticipating what I was opening my mouth to say. 'That doesn't mean they don't have a real sibling bond, Cyn. From what you've told me, it certainly seems like their relationship is complicated, as sibling relationships often are. He might be feeling guilty that Thomas has been disappointed, and at the same time feeling as though he has a lot to prove to you. I'll make sure that your dad goes easy on him.' She winked.

'Thanks.' I sighed, feeling a bit better.

'Listen, you've got to fix your own breakfast today. I totally forgot how much time and effort this bloody soup takes!' She raised her arm to her face, pretending to feel faint.

'Don't worry,' I said, wriggling off the bar stool. 'I'll just grab some toast. I'm not that hungry.' I made my way to the cupboard where the bread was kept.

'Young love, I remember that!' she sighed, before turning the radio back up.

All I could do was laugh.

'Girl, have you seen the time? I'm not changing again!' I barked, propping the phone up on my bookshelf so J could see my outfit properly.

'I don't know, I just feel like it's a little too casual,' she insisted.

'Of course it is to *you*, Miss *Anything-lower-than-a-five-inch-hool-is-flat*,' I shot back.

'Well, some of us ain't been blessed with all that leg, babe,' she said.

This was true. J was barely taller than my mum. No lie, I think she stopped growing in Year Seven. 'Nah, man, I need to be comfortable. Trainers it is. And let's not lie, these are fire,' I said, cocking my foot to the camera to show her my fresh dunks.

'My God, *fine*,' she relented. 'But don't be shocked if he mistakes you for one of the mandem,' she added.

'Mandem?! Do you know where I go to school? There's not another Black boy for miles,' I giggled, stepping back again to give her the full look.

I had decided on mid-wash boyfriend jeans, a grey hoodie, my favourite leather jacket, the black and white dunks, and a small leather crossbody bag, which could only hold essentials but was cute enough that I forgave it.

'I've got to say though, Auntie June came through with the look. Your hair is fire.' She clicked her tongue.

'Now, that we can agree on!' I laughed, walking over to the mirror to check my hair again. The baby hairs were actually laid to death and Mum's gold bamboo earrings that I had been eyeing since I was a little girl – which she'd finally relented and loaned to me – really set the tone. Casual but cute, just how I liked it. I felt like me. And the good thing was, with Isaac I genuinely felt like I didn't have to be anyone else.

'Listen, Craig is trying to call me,' she said.

'Craig who!? Not *Craig* Craig?' I said in shock.

'Mmmhmm,' she said, half sheepishly, half proudly.

My eyes grew wide but I quickly fixed my face. A lot of J's escapades I could overlook but not only was Craig so much older than us and a uni dropout, he was also known for having a lot of girls on the go. Mum's words from earlier flooded my head and I quickly decided to keep my opinions to myself.

'Girl, a bit like this outfit . . . if you like it, I'm cool with it,' I lied.

'And I do! Like him, a lot . . . I think—'

The sound of my doorbell stopped her short.

'Is that yo man?!' she screeched.

'I think so . . .' I whispered, suddenly feeling a little dizzy.

'OK, go – GO – text me, love you – BYE!' she yelled, before hanging up so fast I was left looking at my own reflection.

'Oh, Christ,' I sighed. I couldn't worry about Jadell right now. There would be time for that later. I took one last look at myself in the mirror and then headed downstairs.

I could see Isaac hovering nervously just inside the open front door, both my parents facing him.

He was dressed more casually than he had been at the party.

Less stuffy, more . . . relaxed. He had on dark-green combat pants, a black hoodie and – I couldn't help smiling when I noticed – the same kicks as me, but in green and white. He somehow looked younger than at the party, but also older than he did in his school uniform.

'Good to meet you, young man,' Dad was saying, meeting Isaac's already outstretched hand with his own.

'Good to finally meet you properly as well, Mr Adegoke,' Isaac responded, our last name rolling smoothly off his tongue.

'Mrs Adegoke,' he said to Mum, turning and holding out his hand to her.

'Oh, stop with that nonsense,' Mum said warmly. 'I'm Aunt Veronica to you, and come give me a hug,' she demanded, arms open wide.

Oh god, I wanted the ground to open up and swallow me whole. She used to do this with Big Mike's friends too. *Way* too familiar.

Pulling back, she looked at him. 'You look so familiar!' she exclaimed. 'Doesn't he look familiar, Tunde?' she asked, nudging Dad.

'Hmmm, yes. Like one of Mike's friends, perhaps,' Dad said, shrugging his shoulders. 'What was that tall boy's name – Eric?'

Isaac looked visibly uncomfortable. It was time to intervene. I coughed and everyone turned to look at me. Isaac's eyes grew as wide as his smile.

'All right, all right, can we continue this Spanish Inquisition another time?' I joked. 'I'm hungry,' I lied, trying to get myself and Isaac out of the house. I was still too nervous to think about food.

'Hey,' said Isaac softly, giving me another wide smile. 'I hope you don't mind, Samuel is driving us this afternoon,' he said, looking towards the door.

'Oh, I remember Samuel. Let me just pop out to say—' Dad stopped mid-sentence when he saw the *don't you dare* glare that Mum was throwing him. 'On second thoughts, I have to finish looking over some referrals,' Dad said with a sigh. 'Please pass on my warm wishes, Isaac. I trust you won't have Cynthia home too late?'

'No, of course not. I'll have her back before nine. If that's all right with you, sir?'

'Very well,' Dad said after a moment.

It irked me that Dad wasn't as talkative as he had been with Thomas. And I distinctly remembered him telling Thomas not to call him sir, but he'd let Isaac go on doing it. It made me sad that Dad always wanted to appease white people before making his own feel welcome. But that was a bone to be picked later.

'OK, you crazy kids, have a good time,' Mum said. 'Not too much of a good time though,' she added, pulling me in for an embrace. 'Got your GVM?' she whispered into my ear as she hugged me.

I squeezed her hand and nodded as I pulled away.

'Well, thank you, Mr and Mrs Adegoke,' Isaac grinned shyly.

'Yes, tell your parents – uh – your family, tell them I said hello,' Dad said, fumbling over his words awkwardly.

'I will let them know, sir,' Isaac said, moving aside so I could step through the door first.

'Bye,' I said with a small wave at Mum, before hurrying down the path, not wanting to navigate verbal landmines for a moment longer, Isaac following after me.

Behind us, I heard the door shut, although I didn't have to look over my shoulder to know that Mum would now be running to the nearest window to spy on us.

The car waiting for us was big, black and shiny, like something a popstar or president would be driven around in. It was high off the ground, but a little step revealed itself when Isaac opened the door for me. I felt like I was in a movie – but when it came to how the Goddards could flex I didn't think anything could surprise me any more.

'Thanks,' I said with a sigh, climbing into the back seat. 'Hey, Samuel. It's nice to see you again.' I didn't know why, but something about Samuel made me feel comfortable. Maybe the way he humbled that highty-tighty woman (as my mum would have called her) on the night of the Goddards' party.

'Miss Adegoke.' He smiled broadly, waiting for Isaac to slide in next to me. 'Are we all set, young sir?' he asked Isaac.

'Yes, my G,' Isaac said.

My head snapped round. 'My G?' I giggled.

'Yeah.' Isaac shrugged, smiling. 'Cyn, remember, I had a life before moving out here. Whenever I feel like it's a safe space, I like to be myself,' he said, letting his head flop back into the seat. 'And I always feel like it's a safe space around you.' He turned to look at me and offered me his open palm.

My stomach grew tight again as I placed my hand in his, letting him interlace his warm fingers with my own.

'And can I also say, your hair is fire.' He grinned. I couldn't help but skin teeth. The late night had been worth it. Hopefully, the edge control Auntie June used was as strong as superglue and my baby hairs would respectfully remain laid, at least until after we ate. Once I was home, I didn't care if they wanted to undo themselves.

'Thanks, I thought I would try something a little different.' I shrugged, trying to seem nonchalant.

'Well, it's working.' He smiled and my face warmed under his gaze.

I really couldn't take how perfect he was. The way his skin caught the light. How white and straight his teeth were. And how wavy his trim was.

Mike's hair had been like that. He was very protective of it. Each night he would spend ages meticulously brushing a heavy pomade into it before putting one of his many durags on. Then the next morning he would take it off and like clockwork he would say, 'Jeez, imma leave them seasick.' I shook my head at the sweet memory.

'Relax.' Isaac grinned, clocking my nerves.

'I'm trying to,' I giggled. 'But this is all so . . .'

'Grand? Unnecessary? Extra?' he suggested.

'Um, no, just . . . different,' I said finally.

'I hear you. It took me a while to get used to it too. I was accustomed to having to fight for my life on the number-two bus.' He laughed.

'What? You took the number-two bus too? Shit, how had I never run into you before?' I asked, searching his face to see if it would spark a memory.

'We must have been on different schedules. I would have remembered seeing you,' he said with a smile. 'I was a lot younger then though. But I remember it all. No matter how . . . soft life is now, I remember the harder times . . .' He trailed off. I wanted to ask more, but at that moment the car came to a stop.

'OK, you two, here we are,' Samuel said cheerfully.

The town centre was heaving with people. Parents trying to direct or protect toddlers. Teenagers in small gangs. Old people clinging on to their shopping trolleys for dear life. *So, this is where the action is*, I thought to myself. This was my first time in the centre on a weekend.

'I'll be back at half-eight to pick you both up,' Samuel said.

'Thanks, G,' Isaac said, getting out and jogging around to my side of the car to open the door for me. '*Mademoiselle.*' He bowed slightly and held out his hand.

'*Merci,*' I responded, and I took his hand, allowing him to lead me to the start of my first ever date.

CHAPTER TWENTY-TWO

'OK, come through with the fresh kicks,' he complimented, noticing them for the first time as I climbed out of the car.

'I should say the same to you. I didn't have you down as such a slick dresser,' I admitted, closing the car door behind me.

'If it were down to the Goddards, I'd live in a cashmere pullover and chinos,' he said, suddenly grabbing my waist to stop me walking into the street, just as a car whizzed past.

'Shit,' I gasped, instinctively leaning into him.

'I got you,' he reassured, his hands around my waist leaving me a little light-headed. Or maybe that was the near-death experience.

After a long moment, he let go of my waist, seizing my hand instead. We carefully crossed the road and made our way into the restaurant, waiting at the hostess stand, which was currently unmanned.

'Can I ask you a question?' I asked, still slightly breathless.

'As long as it's not asking to drive you home already, then sure!' He laughed. Then he quickly added, 'I'm kidding, by the way. I understand consent. No means no.'

I playfully punched him in the arm. 'It's not about the date, silly. But the Goddards. Why don't you call them Mum and Dad?' I asked.

There was a slight pause as Isaac caught sight of a waiter across the room and held up his hand in a wave. The waiter smiled and signalled that he'd be right back to seat us.

'Because my adoption situation is . . . complicated. It's not like they copped me as a chubby-cheeked baby who had no memory of anything before they fostered me,' he said. 'I was a full-grown kid, nearly ten. I don't remember my biological mum and dad, but I do remember living in south London. And my brother.' He sighed, looking away quickly. 'I mean, sometimes I slip up and other times I say it just to make them feel good, make them feel better about saving a Black boy from the hood.' He laughed but the smile didn't reach his eyes. 'Don't get me wrong, I owe the Goddards a lot . . . but it doesn't mean I've forgotten where I've come from.'

I so desperately wanted to know more, to know everything. This was the most forthcoming and at ease he had ever been. But I didn't want to rush or pressure him. So I let it go. For the moment.

'Can I help?' a rough voice interrupted.

We both looked over at the same time. A petite white woman was now at the desk, staring at us with a strange look on her face. Her pinched, pained face reminded me of a bird's.

'Errr, yes, well, no,' Isaac answered, visibly flustered. 'I was hoping to grab a table for two.' He smiled.

'We're full,' the waitress said flatly.

I couldn't help but let out a disbelieving laugh. Apart from maybe five other people the place was resoundingly empty.

'We have a lot of bookings today,' she snapped, picking up on the fact that she sounded absurd. 'Why don't you try KFC?

No need to book and I'm sure it will be much more to your fancy.' She smiled coldly.

'Wow, are you mad—' I began, ready to tear her to shreds with my tongue, but Isaac gently put his arm out in front of me, a universal signal for *calm down, I've got this*.

I kissed my teeth but before anything else happened, the waiter who had signalled to Isaac before was now back in front of us.

'Welcome back, Mr Goddard!' he said warmly. The woman's face paled. She had no idea how much this man had saved her life.

'Please, Emidio – it's Isaac,' said Isaac, sounding embarrassed.

I tried to act unimpressed by the fact that he was known by name here, but it *was* slightly intimidating. In this space, he held power. But unlike his brother, he didn't get drunk on it, and that made him even more attractive.

'Ah – I can't, your father would . . .' Emidio acted out having his throat slit. 'And who is this lovely young lady?' he cooed, grabbing two menus and beckoning for us both to follow him. We left the white woman behind without a second glance.

'This is my . . . my friend, Cynthia,' Isaac said slightly awkwardly.

I smiled shyly at Emidio.

'Well, I have to say you are a very lucky young man to have such a beautiful *friend*,' Emidio said, giving me a wink. 'The usual booth is ready – is that OK?'

'All good,' Isaac assured him.

Emidio led us to a corner booth at the back of the restaurant, and Isaac stepped aside to let me slide in first, while Emidio waited. I had never had so much attention on me. I didn't know what to do with myself.

'I'll be back in a moment with some water,' Emidio said, handing us menus.

'Wow.' I exhaled deeply once Emidio was out of earshot.

'What's up?' asked Isaac.

I paused, turning my thoughts over in my head before I decided to say them out loud. 'Let's be honest, where we're from, old girl back there would have got cussed out. Maybe worse. Here, you just waited for that other guy to show up and fix things. It's like, you were . . . protected, I guess, because of the Goddards' wealth and reputation. But that protection disappears as soon as you're somewhere their influence doesn't reach. How does that all feel?' I asked, hoping he could sense that I wasn't trying to pry, but just wanted to understand his life.

He chuckled. 'It feels like I got lucky.' He responded with such speed it was clear that this was something he had thought about before. 'You know, most boys that look like me – fuck it, I don't need to police my chat with you – most *Black* boys, they only have the latter. People only look at them as a problem. They could just be going about their day and bam – they're in the wrong place at the wrong time and they're labelled the bad one – the . . .' He trailed off, nervously toying with the edge of the menu.

I wanted to tell him that I got it, that this was something I understood all too well, but I stayed silent, not wanting to distract him.

195

'As sad as my story is,' he went on after a moment, 'being adopted by the Goddards secured me a different ending. So I'm grateful to God or whoever . . . and I guess also to the fact that the Goddards couldn't have any more children after Thomas, and their willingness to adopt someone older than six months old,' he said with a wry smile. 'It is weird though,' he added, 'to have the woman back there try and check us the way she did, but then less than a minute later to be treated so well by her colleague, who knows me by name and likes to make sure that any member of the Goddard family has their favourite booth. It's a bit of a mind fuck,' he admitted.

I could have listened to him talk for hours.

'But still, like I said, I'm one of the lucky ones,' he finished. 'Damn, it's hot in here.' He stood, pulling his hoodie up and over his head. The front of his T-shirt raised up just enough for me to get a glimpse of a taut and muscular stomach. Now *my* face was becoming hot. I looked away quickly.

When he sat back down, he was closer to me than before, close enough so that our legs touched.

'I am one of the lucky ones,' he repeated, looking at me and reaching out to gently move my braids behind my shoulders.

'Sparkling or still?' Emidio appeared from nowhere with two bottles of water.

'Sparkling,' Isaac and I said in unison.

'Ah, see, you young lovebirds . . . I mean *friends* . . . were meant to be. Are you both ready to order?' he asked.

Ready to order? Hell, I could eat a house. Jadell had said to me that eating a lot in front of a boy made him go off you, and I should only order a salad, but I'd already decided to stop following her rules after the hanging up the phone incident. If Isaac wanted to date me, he would have to get on board with my appetite.

'Ladies first,' Isaac prompted.

'Umm, could I make a request?' I asked shyly.

'Of course, madame!'

'OK, no one judge me . . . but I'm a massive fan of pineapple on my pizza.' I cringed, pretending to hide behind my menu, knowing this was probably the least-popular pizza preference in the world.

'Isaac, will you tell her or shall I?' Emidio asked solemnly.

'Go ahead,' Isaac said, his face unreadable.

'That's Isaac's favourite too,' Emidio whispered to me, beaming as if he were confirming I did indeed possess the winning lottery ticket. 'Though if we were back in Italy, you would both be thrown into the sea,' he added, nudging Isaac's shoulder.

'Nah, you're playing?' I exclaimed, looking from Emidio to Isaac and back again. 'Do you know how many times I've been made to feel as though I'm crazy for that?'

'Now we can be weirdos together,' Isaac said, smiling.

'So one large pineapple pizza?' Emidio confirmed.

'Yes, please,' Isaac and I said in unison.

'Perfect,' he said. 'It will be out shortly.' With a little nod of his head, he took our menus and walked away.

There was a moment of silence. I cast around for something to say, not wanting the conversation to run dry. 'So it's a big deal, Thomas getting a place at Kingwells,' I said finally, interested to know what Isaac thought about it.

'It is and it isn't,' Isaac said with a sigh. 'It was always going to be Kingwells or St James's – I don't think he would have accepted anything less. I mean, don't get me wrong, I don't want to take anything away from him. Thomas is a hard worker and he's put in the effort . . . but I think in some instances he overdoes it.' Isaac shrugged. 'Forgets to just be a normal teen.'

'Oh, I don't know what would possibly give you that idea.' I giggled, thinking of Thomas's formal demeanour when he'd asked my dad if he could take me on a date.

He laughed too. 'It's like, if I'd had the access and privilege he's had since birth, I'd just lap it up. But I think he feels like he always has something more to prove.'

'Yeah, I hear you. So no Kingwells for you?' I asked coyly, hoping I wasn't overstepping a boundary.

He let out a deep sigh. 'I'm not sure, you know. I'll be honest, if I was still back where I'm from I wouldn't have even considered sixth form, let alone uni. I would have had to get a job to help support the fam. So now it feels like I have the chance to think bigger . . . but I'm not even sure how to do that. Mr Goddard could pay for me to go to uni with a flick of his Amex, but I don't know what I'd study. I just have no idea what I want to do with the rest of my life yet. Ya feel me?' he asked, looking at me intently.

'I do. Of course I do. My dad is a surgeon. And you know, I felt it less when my brother was alive. There was so much pressure on *him* to go to university and follow in my dad's footsteps that I was OK with being overlooked a bit. But now it's like, *blam!* All-eyes-on-me type of vibe. I'm not sure about what I want to do or who I want to be yet either. But there is no way my dad is gonna let me get out of higher education. He is Nigerian after all.' I shrugged and reached for my water.

'I hear you. It's mad cos I feel like if I were still in ends it would be like a badge of honour going to uni. A sign to say I made it. But how do you prove you've made it in a world where you already have it made?' he mused, looking at me intently.

Gosh, he was wise. 'That is the question.' I said, trying to avoid his piercing gaze.

'What about you, Cyn? How is all this –' he waved his hand around to help illustrate what he was saying – 'treating you?' I let out a long sigh. 'Remember, you can be honest with me. I'm not *them*,' he said, knowing that I would understand what he meant.

'I know,' I said shyly. *Where do I even begin?* I didn't want our first date to be soured by sombreness, but the truth of how I was feeling was still so complicated.

'Sorry to interrupt.' Emidio had appeared at the side of our booth, saving me from responding, artfully balancing a large pizza tray in one hand.

'No need to apologise!' I exclaimed, genuinely meaning it.

'One large pineapple pizza,' Emidio announced, placing the dish between us.

'Thanks, Emidio,' Isaac said with an embarrassed grin at me.

'Anything else?' the waiter asked cheerfully.

'Not for me. Cyn, you good?' Isaac asked.

'All good,' I assured them both.

'Very well. Please grab my attention if you change your minds,' Emidio said, gliding away from our table.

There was a slightly awkward moment of silence.

'Ladies first.' Isaac smiled, encouraging me to take the first slice.

I smiled back, reaching for the slice closest to me and dragging it on to my plate. Isaac was watching me. All of a sudden, I felt very aware of myself. I sat up a bit straighter. What was my hair doing? Were my baby hairs behaving themselves? Was I sweating too much? Was he not going to reach for some too? Sure, I had eaten in front of him before, but this was different. This felt more . . . intimate. *Just eat the bloody pizza, Cynthia!* I yelled at myself.

Slowly I lifted my pizza and thankfully he turned his attention to grabbing his own slice. He ate like most boys did, unbothered by having an audience, so I relaxed and followed suit, allowing myself to slouch again and really enjoy the food.

'Oh my god, why is this so good, please?' I sighed.

'I know,' Isaac said. 'It's genuinely the best pizza spot north of London. And trust me, Da— Mr Goddard and I have done the legwork.'

I followed his lead and ignored the fact that he had almost said 'Dad', though I noticed it was the second time he'd done something like that. It was the same before, with Mrs Goddard – stopping himself from calling her 'Mum'. I wondered why. Was it loyalty to his biological parents? Or was it a feeling that even after so much time with them, this wasn't his real life? That it never would be?

'Ah, you've got a little something . . .' Isaac gestured to my mouth.

Mortified, I quickly tried to reach for my napkin, but one of his hands, softer and yet bigger than I remembered, was already on my cheek, gently brushing something off the side of my face. I felt like I was dying and being reborn at the same time.

'I told you, I got you,' he said, his tone indicating that he wasn't just talking about the pizza.

'Thanks.' I blushed, trying to ignore the fact that my appetite had immediately left the chat.

He sat back just watching me.

I reached for my water.

'What are you staring at?' I finally asked, starting to get a little uncomfortable.

'Oh, nothing. Just the best thing that's happened to me since I started at Thornton's,' he said, before sitting up straight and reaching for a second slice of pizza.

I cackled a little louder than I'd planned to. 'Rah, man's got bars,' I mocked, hoping a little humour would make me less self-conscious.

'See what I mean? You're pretty and you know how to have a laugh,' he said with a wide smile.

I shrugged, not used to hearing so many compliments about myself and not sure how to respond.

'Molly isn't ugly,' I say without thinking. The moment I mentioned her name I wished I hadn't. Why had I brought her into this?

Isaac kissed his teeth. 'She's not my type,' he said flatly.

'Really?' I asked, quickly snatching a glance at him before focusing my gaze on the bubbles in my sparkling water.

'Not at all,' he said seriously. 'Like, no offence,' he added quickly, as if he were now worried about being secretly recorded.

'It's not like you would be offending *me*,' I said with a smile.

'I know, I just want it to be clear. Molly isn't my type. I like girls how I like my coffee.' He paused. 'Not that I actually drink coffee,' he added after a beat. 'But you get my point, right?' he pressed, a little urgently now. 'I've noticed that we Black boys . . . there is this mad thing that seems to happen. It's as if being able to date someone who doesn't look like you is the ultimate way of saying you made it. Especially if we become famous, like a footballer or rapper or suttin. It's like the moment that happens, we just don't like our own any more. Ya get me?' he finished, sounding more south London than ever before.

I was blown away. This was a conversation me and J had a lot because it was so bait. At this point, Black male public figures weren't even trying to hide it. Mum had taken to calling Auntie June any time she saw a photo of a famous Black man standing with a Black woman rather than a white one in the gossip magazines, that's how rare it was. I was impressed that even though Isaac had been planted into one of the whitest spaces ever, he was still aware of how easy it was to be brainwashed into believing that whiteness was equal to success. But I wasn't about to bestow too much props on him for clocking it.

'I'm a dark-skinned Black girl, Isaac. Of course I get you,' I smiled, keeping my tone light.

'The colour of your skin is one my favourite things about

you,' he said shyly. 'It's beautiful.'

'Awww, stop,' I said, embarrassed. Thankfully that same colour helped camouflage how much I was blushing. I shoved him jokingly in the shoulder.

Swiftly he caught my wrist in his hand and then he placed my hand gently on to the table, letting his rest on top of mine. I felt my heart skip a few beats.

'The sooner you get used to me saying nice things about you, the easier our dates will be,' he said with a shrug.

'Wait, dates? Plural? Boy, who—' The rest of my sentence was swallowed by his lips meeting mine. This kiss felt more purposeful than the kiss by the field. It was almost as if his tongue was trying to say everything he felt. I matched his urgent energy, leaning into him a little more, only pulling back eventually to come up for air.

His eyes looked glassy.

'You were saying?' he mocked.

I kissed my teeth and laughed. 'I was *saying* I need to go to the toilet.' What I really needed was a moment to gather myself.

'OK, cool – just promise me you're not going to do a runner?' he asked, standing up to make room for me to get out from the booth.

'I solemnly swear!' I said, raising a hand as if I was in court.

The sound of his chuckle followed me to the bathroom.

I ran into a cubicle and quickly slammed the toilet lid shut so I could use it as a seat, realising with a smile this was exactly what I'd done on day one at Thornton's too, when I'd first texted J about Isaac. By the time I sat, my phone was in my hand. I quickly swiped away a message from Mum that told me to be safe and not do anything she wouldn't. 'Ewww,' I said to myself, my mind now flooded with images of Mum making out with someone. I started crafting a message to J.

> SOS
> Shit
> I think he is 'The One'
> Really

J would know what I meant by that.

My heartbeat quickened with the realisation that what I'd just typed was true. I really did think he was the guy I could . . . do more with than just kiss.

J responded at lightning speed.

> OHMYDAYS
> CALL ME ASAP

> SOON AS I'M HOME

I put my phone back in my pocket so that I could actually use the toilet.

Coming out to wash my hands, I looked at myself in the mirror. Thankfully, my baby hairs were still behaving themselves. I quickly reapplied some lip gloss and smiled at myself. Maybe I was just gassed by all the compliments Isaac had thrown at me, but I thought I looked the prettiest I'd ever looked in my life.

I made my way back to the table to find Isaac settling the bill. I checked my watch and my heart sank a little. Where had the time gone? My smile dropped further when I realised it wasn't Emidio who was taking Isaac's card for payment, but instead the scrawny blonde who'd been so out of order earlier. She tried not to make eye contact and I tried not to give her a kick behind the knees as I came up to the table.

'Damn, you came back too quick!' Isaac said, as he waited for the receipt.

'What, you were gonna ghost me?' I asked, half joking.

'Nah, Dad taught me to always try and settle the bill discreetly.'

I didn't have to guess which dad he was talking about. Those were some rich-folk manners. I remembered Jadell had once called asking me to transfer her some money cos the boy who had asked her out on a date was insisting she pay half. I'd had no doubt Isaac was going to cover the tab, but it felt good to know that I had my GVM on me, and that I could offer at least. But before I'd even gotten the first words out, Isaac was shaking his head.

'It's my treat,' he said. 'I asked you out, after all. Now, can you pretend you didn't get back here for another minute?'

'Ah, sorry, I'll close my eyes,' I said, momentarily squeezing my eyes shut.

'Here you are,' I heard the blonde woman say stiffly, and I opened my eyes to see her handing the card machine back to him.

'Thank you so much,' Isaac said to her in return, and then added, 'I hope you have the day you deserve.' He stood up to face me as the waitress walked off.

You're more forgiving than me,' I said. 'Ain't *no* way I'd be wishing her well.'

He pulled me towards him so we were able to walk towards the door side by side.

'Cyn, I didn't wish her well.' He was smiling slyly. 'I wished her the day that *she deserved*.'

I giggled as I realised what he'd done. 'Gotcha,' I said, annoyed I hadn't clocked earlier.

At the front of the restaurant he stepped in front of me and held open the glass door.

'I really enjoyed that,' Isaac said, as he fell back into step with me outside.

'Yeah, that pizza was bomb,' I agreed.

There was a moment of silence.

'Well, I wasn't necessarily talking about the food. But yeah, that was OK too,' he said, giving me a teasing nudge.

Damn, I needed to get better at this flirting thing. 'I'm just playing,' I backtracked. 'Of course I meant the company,' I said, nudging him back. 'It just sucks it's home time already.' I was annoyed that I hadn't convinced Mum and Dad to agree to a later time.

'Nah, I get it. Your family have a reason to be protective . . .' He trailed off, looking guilty. 'Sorry,' he quickly added, clearly worried he shouldn't have referenced my past.

'Listen, Isaac, if you wanna chill with me, you're gonna have to take some of your own advice. It's OK to say what you're thinking around me. I know you would never purposefully hurt me,' I said, genuinely believing it.

'Cool.' He smiled widely. 'So I'm thinking for our second date, maybe we focus on dessert?'

Even though I know he meant the food, I still felt a little light-headed.

'I'd like that,' I said. 'I'd like that a lot.'

CHAPTER TWENTY-THREE

By the time Isaac had bid me a kiss-free farewell outside my house, I felt like I was walking on cloud nine.

'I'll call you,' he promised, before turning on his heel and doing a soft jog back to the car.

I was hoping that I would be able to sneak into the house and have at least five minutes by myself to process all that had happened before the interrogation began, but when I opened the front door Mum was standing there waiting to pounce, as if she hadn't moved since I'd left.

'And that's what a true gentleman does,' she clapped gleefully. 'You drop my baby girl right back at the front door!' She squealed, pulling me in for a massive hug.

'Mum!' I moaned, trying and failing to keep my poker face intact.

'Cynthia, my dear, please just allow your mother to have this moment,' Dad called from his office doorway. 'Because anyone would think you had left to visit Mars, such was her anxiety.' He chuckled, tucking his glasses into the neck of his jumper.

'Oh, Tunde, be quiet. This was my daughter's first ever date! What type of mother would I be if I didn't wait impatiently by the front door? It's my one chance.'

There were a few beats of quiet and I knew all three of us were thinking that Mum would never get to tease her son about his first date. Mike had been so dedicated to his studies that it was almost as if even the idea of dating hadn't seemed to cross his mind. Dad had gotten concerned at one point that he was gay and was worried about telling them. I still remember the conversation they'd had.

'Mike, your phone is really blowing up. More girl trouble?' Mum teased as she flipped through one of her many recipe books, checking ingredient lists against what was in the fridge. Mike was sitting at the kitchen island studying, his phone beside him lighting up with messages every few seconds.

'Mum, come on.' He rolled his eyes. 'Blake is having some issues with his girlfriend, that's all.' He sighed. 'You know that's not what I'm on.'

Dad looked up from some work papers he was reading. 'But, ah . . . now, "not what you're on". Do you mean it's not girls you are interested in?' he asked.

Mum coughed as if she had inhaled some dust. I felt my own body grow tense and I paused in the middle of writing a text to Jadell. When I looked at Mike objectively, not as a sister, I had to admit he was handsome. Maybe it was weird he'd never dated anyone, but I'd never even thought he might be gay. If he was though, I was sure this was not the way he wanted to tell us. Would Dad be cool about it if he was?

Mike screwed up his face.

'Listen, as your father,' Dad went on, 'I have to ask . . . so I know how best to support you. A few of your mates are dating but you have *yet to speak of a special lady. I know I'm old and from a very different place . . . but it's fine with me, whoever you might want to date,' he finished awkwardly.*

Mike broke into a smile, easing the tension all round.

'Thanks, Dad. But no, I'm not gay. I like girls. I just don't think I'm ready to date yet. At least let me be financially stable enough to buy her ice cream,' he joked, turning his attention back to his phone.

'That's my boy,' Dad said, clearly happy that his education was only for theory, not practice.

So right then, I had to acknowledge how this was a big moment for Mum as well as me. I tried not to let the weight of inheriting the responsibilities of the firstborn crush me.

'So how was it? Was this boy as polite as Thomas?' Dad asked.

I rolled my eyes and didn't try to hide it. 'Dad, his name is Isaac. And yes, in fact, he was very polite.' I couldn't stop myself from smiling.

'Hmph, well, I'm happy to hear it,' he said, giving me a nod.

'Will there be a second date?' Mum pressed, looking at me as if I was the main character from a soap opera.

I shrugged. 'I hope so.' I kicked off my trainers as Mum opened her mouth to ask another question, but thankfully just then the oven timer began to wail.

'Oh my god, the black cake!' Mum cried, dashing towards the kitchen.

'I say run before she comes back,' Dad suggested with a smile.

'Thanks, Dad.' I said, not waiting to be told twice. I took the stairs two at a time, hurrying into my room and quickly closing the door behind me.

As soon as I was alone, I broke out into a happy dance. A proper arch your back, cock your bum, carnival-type whine. I was so elated. The feeling of my vibrating phone broke me out of my trance. I smiled even harder when I pulled it out of my pocket and saw that it was Isaac. I was going to wait for a few rings to pass so I didn't seem too eager, when I remembered my vow not to follow any more of J's tips and tricks. I quickly pressed the green symbol.

'Hi,' I offered breathlessly.

'Uh, hi . . . Are you OK? You sound busy?' he asked suspiciously.

'Um, yeah, I'm fine,' I said. The truth was, I was ecstatic. 'Just out of breath from the stairs. Gotta get myself on one of those Thornton's sports teams,' I joked, and he laughed, the warm sound of it against my ear making me breathless all over again.

'OK, listen,' he said. 'On a serious tip, it occurred to me that I didn't ask you the most important question of all.' He sounded nervous.

'Oooookaaaayyyy,' I said, now curious.

'Um . . .' he began, and then trailed off.

'Isaac – spit it out!' I said a little too loudly, beginning to worry. I had become accustomed to getting bad news. My only requirement now was that the proverbial plaster was ripped off quickly.

'Jeez, I'm coming,' he said with a laugh, and his teasing tone made me relax just a bit. It couldn't be too bad, if he was still laughing. 'I wanted to know,' he said, 'before we went on another date . . . ifyouwouldbemygirlfriend?' He spoke the last six words so quickly it was as if they were threatening to blister his mouth.

I let the breath I didn't even know I'd been holding out, all my remaining worry floating away with it.

'Cyn? Are you there?' His voice moved away from the speaker, presumably to check if the call was still connected.

'Yeah . . . I mean, *yes*. Yes. I would love that. To be your girlfriend. That would be . . . great. Really great,' I finished, my mouth still working to catch up with my brain.

'Ah, phew. I thought you were gonna tell me that I'd got this all wrong. This is the first time I've done this, you know.' I could practically hear his shy smile through the phone.

'Me too,' I said softly. I was in awe of how easy it was to be honest with him. No pretence.

'OK . . . well. I can't wait to see you on Monday. Sleep well, Cyn.'

'You too.' I grinned, waiting for him to end the call this time. The moment I was sure he'd gone, I threw my phone on the bed and proceeded to dance as if I were on a soca float at Notting Hill Carnival.

A few minutes later, feeling as though my heart was going to burst through my ribcage, I flopped backwards on to my bed and let out a long, happy sigh. I reached for my phone to call J but before I could, it began to buzz and flash with her name.

'Speak of the devil!' I exclaimed.

'And the bitch will be there!' Jadell cackled in response. 'Girl – what happened?! I was starting to worry that you found yourself in a proper *Get Out* situation. Like the white mum in an armchair hypnotising you with some peppermint tea.'

'Girl, bye,' I laughed, although to be fair, the settings at the party hadn't been too far off. 'No, listen, just listen to what happened!' I said, still slightly out of breath.

'WHAT IS IT?! SPEAK UP NOW!' J demanded.

'HEASKEDMETOBEHISGIRLFRIEND ANDISAIDYES!' I spoke so quickly I almost bit my tongue.

I could no longer make out what J was saying, but instead I could hear the air whipping and a thumping noise, as if she were jumping up and down with the phone in her hand. 'Oh my days, OH MY DAYS!' she yelled, her voice coming back into its fullness as she put the phone back to her face. 'Oh, Cyn, I'm so happy for you. We can go on double dates soon!' she said.

'Yeah, soon!' I said, without missing a beat, although I had no intention of going through with the idea. Isaac wasn't at all like the boys J kicked it with and I couldn't see a double date going well. But I didn't want her to think that I was coming across all judgemental.

'Who would have thought that your man was out there in foreign lands. This is so mad!'

She was right. I tried not to think too much about the instances that had led to me landing at Thornton's and meeting Isaac – no, meeting *my boyfriend*. Even just saying it in my head was going to take some getting used to.

'Anyways, I gotta run,' J said. 'Later, gator . . . or should I say later, *girlfriend*!' She squealed once more before hanging up the phone.

I threw the phone on the bed and turned to look at myself in the mirror on my vanity, still unable to stop smiling. It seemed as if my smile had finally reached my eyes again.

There was life after death after all. And I wasn't mad at it.

The next week at school felt strange. Although I was sure Isaac hadn't told anyone about us, whenever there were other people around it felt as if we were on a stage, as if the entire school was aware that we were now a couple.

The best times were when Isaac and I were alone together. We had started spending our free periods tucked away in the library and on Thursday afternoon I finally asked Isaac about it. 'Do you feel like everyone's just been staring at us this week?' I asked in a whisper.

'No more than when they were staring at us before, babe.' He shrugged, sinking himself further into the bean bag we were sharing. He had taken to calling me babe when no one else could hear, which always made my heart do a little jump. I liked how intimate it felt.

'What about Thomas being right there when we came in today after lunch?' I pressed. 'That was weird, wasn't it? Like he'd been watching for us or something.' We had run into Thomas on our way back into the main building after having lunch on the field again earlier that day.

'He's being his normal self at home,' Isaac said with another shrug.

I chewed on my lip. When it came to Thomas, my intuition was still nagging me but considering that Isaac was saying everything was cool, I decided to let it go. Didn't want to upset the apple cart, as Mum would have said, when things should be left well alone.

CHAPTER TWENTY-FOUR

Friday morning I woke up to a series of texts from Isaac.

> Babe I won't be in today. Got an appointment to go 2.
> Do you want to go to the cinema tomorrow?
> I will even watch a romcom
> Xxx

I lay in bed for a moment, staring at his texts. I was a bit annoyed he hadn't given me a heads-up earlier in the week. Unless it was a last-minute appointment. But then, what sort of appointment could it be? Not with his GP because he had been fine yesterday and, anyway, getting a same-day doctor's appointment was harder than a fried dumpling. I figured if it was anything serious he would tell me, and I *was* excited at the thought of spending time with him at the cinema, away from prying eyes, so I decided to suppress my irritation and curiosity.

> Yes :)
> Don't worry, I like movies with fight scenes
> X

With Isaac not in school the day seemed to drag. It occurred to me that since I'd agreed to be his girlfriend, I had subconsciously stopped investing time in making friends with anyone else. While I would never have admitted it, I did feel a little lonely without him by my side. But I had never been a begfriend and I wasn't gonna start being one now, so I sucked it up and focused on how happy I would be when I saw him the next day. By the time I got in from school I was bubbling with so much excitement for our second date that when Mum placed dinner in front of me, I wasn't even hungry.

'Hm, I remember those days,' Mum said with a laugh, noticing my lack of appetite.

'What days?' I asked, trying to play it cool.

'The days of young love!' she sang, leaning over the island pretending to be a performer. 'I was so in love with your dad in the beginning that I couldn't eat; the butterflies kept my tummy full.'

'Only in the beginning?' Dad asked, appearing in the kitchen doorway.

'Yeah, back when I was young and knew no better,' Mum said with a wink to me.

'Well, I would have to say, *I* firmly disagree. I'm more in love with you now than ever.' He smiled broadly, pulling Mum in for a hug.

I made pretend-vomiting sounds, but secretly, seeing them get along made me feel as if everything were right with the world. Even if it was a bit embarrassing.

'Oi, I'll remember to make those sounds when you marry Isaac,' Mum said, pointing at me.

Just the mention of his name made the butterflies increase.

'Aht, aht! No one is thinking of marriage just yet, V. Let her studies be her Prince Charming, please,' Dad said. 'She's got GCSEs next year, and after that her A levels. If she's going to get into Kingwells she needs to apply herself.'

That was my cue to exit. I really didn't want to have this whole higher-education conversation right now. I was still so unsure of what I wanted to do and it felt like everyone at Thornton's was already locked into the plans their parents had for them, which made me feel even more pressure. I slid off the stool and made a half-hearted excuse about retiring to my room to do some coursework.

'That's my girl!' Dad shouted after me as I made a hasty exit. I couldn't help but laugh at his cheerleading.

Once I was in my room, I decided to focus on tomorrow's outfit rather than homework. It was Friday night, after all. I knew that I didn't *need* to dress up for Isaac – he'd been into me when I was wearing my school uniform – but I also didn't want to get caught slipping. Rifling through my clothes for an outfit I was happy with took longer than I expected, because by the time I was done it was gone eleven.

I yawned, realising that I was pretty tired. Unsurprising, really, given how hard I was working at school to keep up with Thornton's standards. I carefully placed my top-three outfit options on my desk, pushed the remaining mountain of clothes from the bed on to the floor and got busy getting ready for bed.

By the time I'd brushed my teeth and put my head tie on, I barely had the energy to scroll through Insta. Just as I went to plug my phone into charge, I got a text from Isaac.

218

I've got to tell you sumthing
But it can wait until tomorrow
Sleep well
Xxx

For some reason, Thomas's warning came rushing to the front of my brain.

Isaac isn't telling you everything, Cynthia. You don't know who he really is.

I shoved the memory to the back of my long line of thoughts. Whatever it was, we could work through it. I could hear Mum's advice echoing through my head: *Always go with the good boy, the one who treats you like you matter.*

Whatever he wants to tell me, we'll work through it, I thought. *He treats me like I matter. And we like each other enough to find a way to make it work.* I yawned again and this time I let my eyes fall shut.

Before I even opened my eyes the next morning, I felt the warm rays of the sun caressing my face. In my haste to get to bed, I'd forgotten to close my blinds. For a few moments, the new morning haze made me forget what was happening that day. I just had a vague sense of being excited about something. Then the fact that I had my second date with Isaac came rushing back and suddenly the butterflies were fluttering in full force again. I sat up quickly, snatching my phone off the charger. I was pleasantly surprised to see a message from Isaac waiting for me. I checked the time – it was only 8.17 a.m.

Did this guy ever sleep? I smiled to myself and slid the message open.

> Movie starts at 2 & should be done by 4
> I will come get U at 1
> Wanna go get ice cream after?

His messages seemed off. There was no 'good morning' and no 'babe'; not even a 'X'. I decided to match his energy.

> Kk

For a while after sending it, I watched the screen, but there was no sign of him typing anything back. Maybe I'd been too low-key. Perhaps I shouldn't have matched his energy after all. I sighed and pulled myself out of bed, immediately stumbling upon the mound of clothes I hadn't put away last night.

The coldness in Isaac's last message had unsettled me but I was determined to shake it off. I put some music on and decided to tackle the clothes before Mum came in unannounced and promptly had a heart attack. That took a little longer than I expected and by the time I went downstairs, Mum had already left to go food shopping. I could hear Dad's voice from behind his office door. Thankful that I would be able to eat without any prying eyes or comments about my love life, I headed into the kitchen. As I ate my toast, I sent J some pictures of my top-three outfit choices and eagerly waited for her response. Within minutes she messaged back.

> It's deffo number 3.
> Number 1 is an outfit only fit for gardening.
> 2 would be better in the bin LOL.

I kissed my teeth and laughed. I could always count on Jadell to be honest.

I was heading back to my room just as Mum came in with the shopping, huffing and puffing dramatically.

'Need some help, Mum?' I asked.

'Well, since you're here, yes,' she answered brightly, mysteriously no longer out of breath.

I waited for her to turn her back before rolling my eyes, then bent down and lifted the bags that she'd left by the door and waddled into the kitchen with them. A moment later, she joined me with some more, heaving them on to the kitchen island.

'Mum, you know there is now this thing called home delivery, right?' I asked.

'Cha. But I like to go in and actually squeeze the fruits and check the use-by dates. And speaking of dates,' she said slyly, 'what time is Isaac picking you up today?'

I felt my tummy grow tight. 'One o'clock.'

'OK, good, that will give me time to spruce the place up a bit,' she said, looking around.

'Mum, you ain't gotta do all that,' I moaned. 'The house looks fine.'

'Your dad told me how they live. I don't want people thinking we don't take pride in our home.'

I was genuinely taken aback. I'd never heard Mum sound quite so much like, well . . . Dad. But I guessed she was starting to realise how different things were here. Isaac picking me up with a chauffeur for our first date probably hadn't helped. Perhaps that's where her insecurity was coming from.

'Mum, Isaac used to live near our area. Before he was adopted, obviously. You don't need to do anything special for him.' I hoped that would calm her down.

'Did he really?' she asked, sounding surprised. 'You should have said. Now I think about it, I'm pretty sure I've seen his mum before at June's salon. Maybe that's why he looked familiar.'

I wanted to start getting ready, so I didn't get into how that was actually impossible given the fact she was dead.

'I'm going to head upstairs now,' I advised, slowly backing out of the kitchen.

'OK, my love. Don't forget the deodorant. You know how much you sweat when you're a bit nervous.'

'YES, MUM!' I yelled from the stairs, annoyed and grateful in equal measure. I could always count on Mum to simultaneously have my back and humble me.

The doorbell went while I was still upstairs getting ready.

I hastily checked my phone. Isaac was five minutes early.

'Isaac,' I heard Mum say cheerily a moment later. 'Come in, come in. Stop acting like a garden gnome.' I cringed at her cheesy joke.

Then I heard Dad's deeper tones. 'Hello, young man. Pleasure to meet you again.'

'Hello, Mr Adegoke.' Even the sound of Isaac's voice brought a smile to my face. I took one last look at myself in the mirror before deciding to go and save my boyfriend from further embarrassment.

'Oh, please, call me Tunde,' I heard Dad say as I started down the stairs. That made me smile. Perhaps he was finally allowing himself to see Isaac and Thomas as equals. That or maybe Mum had given him a firm talking-to.

I gave Isaac a clumsy one-armed hug when I reached him, pulling away quickly as he tried to give me a kiss. I could feel Dad's sharp eyes on us and I was *not* ready for kissing in front of my parents.

'I missed you at school yesterday,' I said to Isaac, trying to distract Dad.

'Yeah, sorry about that. I went to visit a college in Wallbridge,' he said.

I wished I hadn't said anything. Dad didn't need more reminders that people in my year were starting to look at colleges.

'Hmm, I know Wallbridge. A strange place to further your education,' Dad said, sounding curious.

'Yeah, it's not Kingswell, I know,' Isaac said with a small smile. 'But I have some . . . family . . . blood family . . . out that way, so Mum and Dad – the Goddards – are trying to support me being near them.' He looked a little sad.

If it wasn't for being in the presence of Mum and Dad, I would have thrown my arms around him and given him a massive hug. But instead I pretended to look at the time on my phone.

'We should head out. Shouldn't we?' I asked, turning to Isaac. 'I don't want to miss the trailers. They're the best part,' I added, gently tugging his sleeve. Thankfully, he quickly cottoned on and let himself be pulled out of the door. I waved goodbye to my parents and half jogged out to the massive black car in the drive.

Isaac opened the door for me and I hopped in, happy to finally be out from under the gaze of my parents.

'Hi, Samuel,' I said, sliding across the seats so Isaac could climb in after me.

'Miss Adegoke,' Samuel replied with a smile. 'And how are you today?'

'Much better now I'm away from my parents, actually,' I said. Samuel chuckled.

'They just want the best for you,' Isaac said, gently squeezing my hand.

'I know.' I sighed, turning my palm upwards so he could hold it properly. I so badly wanted to kiss him, but it felt too awkward with Samuel right there in the front.

'So . . . Wallbridge?' I asked Isaac, wondering why he'd never mentioned it. 'I know I've only been your girlfriend for . . . a couple of minutes, but a heads-up would have been nice.' Was I the only one of us already thinking about what would happen when we both left Thornton's? Was it too early to be talking about that, thinking about where he'd be, where I'd be, whether we'd stay together . . . ? My words had come out a little more sternly than I intended, and I felt

224

his body grow tense beside me.

'Yeah, about that. Nothing has been decided yet, but now they know where Thomas is headed, our parents want to ensure that I don't feel abandoned . . . again,' he said quietly.

I immediately felt awful. I had to remember that we weren't just two carefree young teenagers who went on dates and had whole uncomplicated lives in front of us. That in fact our paths had only crossed because we had *both* been through traumatic experiences. I decided to ease off a little.

'Sorry,' I muttered sheepishly.

'No worries,' he said, and he pulled me closer against him.

We sat in comfortable silence until we pulled up at the town centre. Isaac got out of the car and came around to my side to open my door. The car seemed even higher than I remembered.

'I swear this car has grown,' I joked.

Isaac laughed.

'What?' I asked, allowing him to take my hand as I jumped down.

'Sam had the wheels changed. They're bigger than the ones that were on before, so this bulletproof bad boy *is* actually a little higher off the ground,' Isaac explained, firmly closing the door behind me and waving goodbye to Samuel.

'Bulletproof?' I squealed. A few pedestrians turned to look at me.

Isaac shrugged. 'That's what Mr Goddard says anyway. You never know with him. He could be telling the truth.'

I faked a shiver.

'Come on, Cyn. The way I see it, you can't be as rich as the

Goddards and not have someone wanting you in an urn. Where we're from, plenty have enemies and have lost their lives for a lot less,' he said matter-of-factly.

I knew he was right. We had both come up in environments where people had been attacked and even killed for a fraction of what the Goddards were worth. But something about that reality still made me uncomfortable.

He pulled me in for a hug,

'But I promise you're safe with me,' he whispered.

I genuinely felt it.

We crossed the road to the cinema, and as we did, I caught sight of a massive poster for a new movie called *Things I Never Wanted to Tell You*. It looked like a horror, which meant I was very much *not* the target audience, but spotting it reminded me of the text he'd sent me last night.

'So what was it you wanted to tell me?' I pressed as we stepped into the cinema.

There was a slight change in atmosphere.

After a moment of silence he said, 'You know what, it can wait till later. Let's just have a good time.' He tried to smile but I could see the tension in his brow.

I shrugged, hoping it would come across as nonchalant. I *really* wanted to know but I also didn't want to totally disrupt the mood.

He looked up at the large monitor that was displaying a list of films and their screen numbers. 'We're in screen three. I've already got the tickets, so what do you want to eat?' he asked as we neared the popcorn and pick 'n' mix.

'Um, I'm not that hungry,' I lied. I didn't want him to

have to pay for my food too, when he'd already treated me to the tickets.

He turned to me and raised his eyebrow. 'Cyn,' he prompted.

'OK . . . the popcorn smells good,' I said, laughing.

Thankfully he laughed too. 'Well, I'm a salt and sweet kinda bruddah,' he revealed.

'No way, fam! Me too!' For a second, I was a little embarrassed that I'd slipped into my south London slang so casually in public, but Isaac just smiled and put his arm around me. 'That's my girl,' he said, squeezing my shoulder.

'A large salt and sweet, please,' Isaac said, beaming at the girl behind the counter who looked like she was around the same age as us. When she clocked Isaac, she gazed at him the same way all the girls at Thornton did – like she'd happily give him anything he asked for.

'One large popcorn, coming right up.' She smiled sweetly at Isaac, not looking in my direction.

I nearly kissed my teeth, but I didn't want her to know she'd rankled me. A few moments later, she came back and handed him the popcorn, her hand brushing against his. Isaac pulled the box towards him quickly, turning to me.

'Babe, did you want a drink?' he asked, reaching for my hand.

The girl looked annoyed, her smile becoming more of a sneer. The butterflies in my stomach returned as Isaac pulled me closer to him.

'Sure, I guess I'm a little thirsty,' I said, smiling at the girl. *Not as thirsty as some*, I thought, as Isaac ordered drinks for us both.

Thoroughly dismissed, the girl grabbed our sodas and turned

to the next customer without a word.

There was a lanky, pimple-faced young man at the door to screen three, checking tickets. We waited as he waved the people ahead of us through, barely glancing at them.

'Tickets, please,' he barked when we reached him.

My guard immediately went up. I wanted to say something – ask him why he was singling us out when he had let those other people breeze on by – but Isaac already had our tickets ready. He solemnly thrust them towards the guy, who shone a small torch on them, inspecting them way longer than necessary.

'Good, all in order,' he said, confirming what we already knew.

This time I did kiss my teeth.

'Cyn, it's OK,' Isaac said, holding the door to our screen open for me. 'Let's just have a good time.'

I took a deep breath. He was right – I didn't want our second date to include me cussing out the self-righteous ticket boy. The trailers were still playing as we found our seats and got settled. There was only a handful of other people in the auditorium. Whenever Jadell and I went to the cinema in ends, we always ended up sitting in front of a bunch of guys who would throw popcorn in our direction, trying to get her attention.

'Please remember to silence your phones,' a faceless voice ordered as the trailers finished.

When I pulled my phone out to make sure it was on silent, I saw I had a few messages. Geeked-out ones from Jadell. One from Mum checking in. And then a stream of them from Thomas.

READ THIS NOW was the first text preview. I had no doubt

228

he knew I was out with Isaac today and was likely trying to distract me from the date. I quickly opened his messages. They were pictures, but they wouldn't load as it seemed what all cinemas had in common was poor reception. Cha, Thomas could wait. It was probably a meme or something.

'All good?' Isaac asked, slyly throwing his arm over the back of my seat.

'Yep,' I smiled, stuffing the phone back into my bag and turning to face him. His mouth was very close to mine.

'You?' I whispered.

'Well . . . there is one thing that could make me better,' he said with a grin.

'Really?' I asked, inching my face towards his.

He closed the distance, pressing his lips to mine. All the kisses before this one had felt like child's play, a warm-up. This was burning, hungry. Lips parted ways to make room for tongues. Our teeth clashed a few times, but I didn't care. The sound of the movie starting was the only reason we caught our breath.

'Much better,' Isaac said, allowing himself to slouch deeper into the seat.

The film was OK. To be honest, I wasn't that focused on it. The true standout moments were our continuous stolen kisses. And when I started to feel sleepy, I allowed my head to fall on to Isaac's shoulder. He adjusted his position to make it more comfortable and then gently kissed my forehead. I wanted to pinch myself. I had only seen this kind of date in movies. It dawned on me that even Jadell might not have experienced a truly romantic moment like this, and that made me sad.

Two hours later, we tumbled out of the cinema drunk on kisses and Coke.

'You see, what I don't understand is why they always insist on the same dead storyline,' Isaac remarked.

'Fear, innit. Trying to make sure that the majority of the audience are happy,' I said.

'I'm definitely happy,' he smiled, pulling me in for a hug.

'Me too,' I replied, leaning into him.

The ice-cream place was within the same shopping centre, just a three-minute walk away. We strode hand in hand, and I allowed myself to actually feel it, the happiness. I hadn't felt like this – this light, this at ease – since before Big Mike died. In those earlier, darker days when everything, even breathing, felt like a chore, I couldn't have imagined what life could look like now. Maybe leaving the Big Smoke hadn't been such a bad idea after all.

My phone was vibrating again. I tugged on Isaac's arm, signalling for him to hold on a minute.

I pulled my phone out – it was Thomas again. For fuck's sake. I sighed and stuffed the phone back into my bag.

Isaac eyed me suspiciously. 'Everything OK?' he asked, seeming genuinely concerned.

'Uh, yeah, just Dad messaging me about stuff that can wait,' I lied, hooking my arm around his. 'Man, I'm so excited about ice cream. Good shout,' I added.

'I got you,' he said, pulling the door to the dessert parlour open.

As we walked up to the counter, I swallowed and decided to just ask what had been on my mind all afternoon.

'So what is it you wanted—' I started, trying to keep my tone light.

'Damn, I've really got to go for a wee!' he said all of a sudden, cutting me off mid-sentence. 'Hold that thought, yeah?'

'Uh . . . OK.' I giggled nervously. He was really making me wonder now. Isaac was clearly trying to avoid having this conversation, so why had he brought it up in the first place?

I watched his tall and muscular frame head to the bathroom and let out a long, satisfied sigh. I wished he would just tell me. I liked him so much. There wasn't anything he could say that would change that, so what was the drama about?

I peered into the freezer, checking out the flavour options while I waited for him to come back, and suddenly remembered all the messages on my phone.

I went into my bag and pulled it out.

At the top was another new message from Thomas.

I TOLD HIM IT WAS UNFAIR TO YOU was all I could see on the preview.

The next preview said **I WARNED HIM TO NOT LEAD YOU ON LIKE THIS**

I opened up my messages and this time the pictures he'd sent before loaded. It looked like images of a letter. I double-clicked on the first one, and used my thumb and forefinger to zoom in.

In the top right-hand corner was an address.

'HMP Wallbridge . . .' I mumbled to myself – so it was a letter from someone in prison. I thought of the letter I'd seen when I snooped at the Goddards' party. Was this a response to that letter, the one I'd seen Isaac writing to his brother? Maybe Thomas thought I had no idea Isaac's brother was in prison. But

I already knew that and didn't care. It didn't mean anything about who Isaac was.

I began to read it.

Yo little bro,

So it was from his brother. This was private, and I didn't need to read it. Isaac would tell me about his brother when he was ready. I went to close it, but then I saw my name and I stopped, my heart pounding. I went back to the beginning of the sentence with my name in it.

You have to tell Cynthia. I didn't kill him. I'm trying to fight the case now. What if I get out? Surely you won't hide me? Mum would turn in her grave.

It felt as if I were being pulled through a drain in slow motion.

I could still hear the tinny background music and the chatter of the boy behind the counter with another customer, but it sounded far away. It felt as though if I screamed no one would hear me. My mind began to move and shift like a Rubik's cube. Memories, now 3D squares, rearranging themselves, trying to make all the sides of this puzzle look the same.

I hastily opened all the other messages Thomas had sent me. There were at least a dozen.

Same handwriting.

Same prison address.

Signed by Israel.

Isaac's brother.

Who was in prison for murder.

A murder he said he didn't commit.

That somehow had something to do with me . . .

I felt the salt and sweet popcorn coming up my windpipe – I thought I was going to be sick. I felt myself slump against the ice-cream cabinet, my legs no longer working to hold me up.

'Cyn! Are you OK?' Isaac's voice pulled me back into reality. He rushed towards me, trying to help me stand.

'DON'T TOUCH ME!' I yelled. 'DON'T TOUCH ME!'

I watched as first confusion and then horror swept across Isaac's face as he realised what I now knew: his brother killed Mike.

'Cyn. Please, please hear me out. I wanted to tell you. I didn't mean for this to happen. For me to fall in love with you . . . Thomas swore he would give me more time,' he gabbled desperately.

I wasn't even listening; I was trying not to hyperventilate.

'YOUR BROTHER KILLED MY BROTHER!' I shrieked, silencing the room.

'It's not that simple!' Isaac begged, following me to the door.

I began to jog now, barely able to see through the tears streaming down my face.

'Cynthia!' Isaac shouted as I shoved my way past a woman entering with a buggy. 'Cyn!' I heard once more, as I began to sprint through the shopping centre.

Once I made it through the automatic doors and on to the road, I threw up all over my new kicks.

'Aw, shit, man, that's disgusting,' a white teenage boy heckled.

'Go. Fuck. Your. Self,' I responded, in between heaving.

233

Once it had all come up, I staggered around. Just across the road was a taxi rank. I shot across without looking. A horn blared loudly but I didn't bother to turn around.

'TAXI!' I yelled to the first car in line.

'Jesus, are you all right?' the taxi driver asked, unable to hide both his concern and repulsion at the smell of sick.

'No!' I cried. 'Please will you take me?'

'Get in, get in,' he said after a moment, taking pity on me. 'Have you been attacked?' he asked, looking back at me, worried.

'Not exactly,' I sobbed.

'All right, love, where do you want to go?' he asked gently.

'Home,' I whispered between sobs, knowing that the address I was about to give wasn't the home I wanted to go to at all.

CHAPTER TWENTY-FIVE

I let my body fall to one side and my head landed on my handbag on the seat, like it was a pillow. Someone was blowing up my phone and the bag was vibrating, sending rhythmic pulses through my head.

I had to be dreaming.

My mind raced through every interaction I'd had with Isaac from the first day we'd met. Had he known who I was from the very beginning? Had everything he'd said to me been a lie? I thought of how Thomas had warned me about Isaac. He'd known. How many other people knew? And what had Isaac meant when he'd said, 'It's not that simple'?

It seemed crystal clear to me.

What would I tell Mum and Dad?

I let all of these questions rattle around in my head as the taxi sped towards home.

'All right, love, here we go,' the driver said softly a short while later, interrupting my still-racing thoughts.

I slowly raised my head. I was home. I fished around in my bag for the GVM money Mum had given me before my first date with Isaac.

'Sorry, I don't have anything smaller,' I whispered between sniffles, handing him the fifty-pound note.

'No, you're all right, love,' he said, pressing it back into my hand. 'I've got a kid your age. I'm just doing what I wish anyone would do for mine. You OK to get in on your own? Will someone be home?'

'Yes,' I said, trying not to cry, his kindness prompting even more tears. 'Thank you so much.' I attempted a smile then opened the car door and clumsily tumbled out.

I wasn't even halfway up the drive when the front door opened and Mum came sprinting towards me. I quickly tried to pat my face dry of tears. But my trainers were still stained with sick.

'CYNTHIA! DID HE HURT YOU?!' she shrieked, shaking me as if she were trying to expel a demon. 'DID HE HURT YOU?!' she repeated.

I shook my head. 'Not physically,' I sobbed, allowing all of my body weight to fall on to her.

She momentarily staggered but quickly steadied herself and supported me into the house.

'We realised about twenty minutes ago. The moment the penny dropped, we tried calling, but you didn't answer,' she said, her voice trembling with worry as we both stumbled into the living room.

'Here, sit down,' she ordered, guiding me to the sofa.

'I don't understand . . .' I said, my voice raspy. 'What penny?'

The sound of Mum's phone ringing interrupted me.

'Yes, she's here, she's here,' she said into the phone.

I could hear Dad's voice on the other end.

'She's OK. Yes, come back. Love you too.' Mum hung up and came to sit on the edge of the chair opposite me. 'Jesus,

Mary and Joseph,' she said with a sigh. 'It was what he said about Wallbridge that made me suspect. That place is a no-man's land, but it just so happens to be the town where your brother's murderer is in prison. Once you both left, something in my spirit wouldn't rest. That, plus the fact he looked so familiar. It kept bugging me. And then just like that, that . . . *thug's* smug face came racing back into my memory. The way he looked in that dock.' She looked out of the window, wiping tears from her eyes. 'I went straight to your dad with my suspicions. He got hold of your uncle Dennis, who was able to find out that Israel had a brother who'd been adopted by a white family when he was a child. No more information than that, but I ain't no fool. I knew it was him. Cyn, we were so worried about you. I haven't been that scared since . . .' She trailed off.

'He wouldn't have hurt me,' I whispered, confused by the fact that I truly believed it.

Mum slowly raised her head. 'Do you know what his brother did to Mike?' she said sharply, not waiting for an answer before continuing. 'Of course you don't, because we protected you from that. Lord knows if I'd had a crystal ball your ass would have been at that trial, day in and day out, listening to how many times Mike was stabbed, kicked, spat on, so I wouldn't have to hear *you* defending his killer's brother!'

I flinched at the thought. Tears were now mixing with snot. I wiped my face with my sleeve.

'He's lied to you from day one. And you have the gall – no, the *audacity* – to tell me that you *know* he wouldn't have hurt you?' She'd stood up and was towering over me, then she kissed her teeth and walked away. 'No sah, the likkle kisses and feel ups mus' ah send yuh head mad ta rhatid,' she spat, walking towards the window. 'Dem fucking apples don't fall far from its tree. If 'im breddah can be heartless enough to kill, then so can he,' she concluded, looking back towards me with eyes filled with fire.

I hung my head, hiding my eyes. Isaac and Israel were two separate people; why should Isaac be painted as guilty purely by genetic association? And yet, my stomach churned as Mum's words about Mike's death echoed in my mind. How could I ever look at Isaac the same way again, knowing what his brother had done to mine? Almost as painful was the fact that I had opened up my heart to him, and he had been lying to me the entire time.

In some ways, maybe Mum was right.

The sound of Dad's car pulling into the driveway caught my attention. I heard a car door slamming and his footsteps running towards us, before the door flew open.

'Veronica! Cynthia!' he yelled, sounding panicked.

'In here,' Mum called to him.

'Oh God, oh God.' Dad rushed into the room and immediately got on his knees in front of me. He put both of his hands on my head and began to pray in Yoruba, interspersed with sentences in English.

'It is well with you!'

'It is my enemy that will worry.'

'I decree and declare every bad spirit that has been sent to seek and destroy be returned to sender in Jesus's name!'

I hadn't seen Dad pray like this since Big Mike was killed. As much as I wanted to run to my room and cry, I remained still, obliging Dad's need to feel as though his flurries of prayers could somehow make this situation better.

When he finished, he took both my hands in his and looked into my eyes. 'Thank God he did not hurt you.'

I didn't even try to contradict it this time.

'Don't worry, we will get you out of Thornton's in no time. I've already got Uncle Dennis helping us with a recommendation for Denbey's,' Dad said.

'What?' I cried. This was all happening so fast.

'I won't have you around the devil for a moment longer,' Dad said, rising to his feet.

Numbly, I stood, mumbling something about going to my room, and then I fled, half running, half tripping up the stairs, desperate to be alone. Opening my bedroom door, I sank to the floor with my back to the wall and let the tears flow freely. I kicked off my filthy trainers and used my feet to push them out of sight. On any other day, I would have started a cleaning routine on them, but today was today and nothing seemed to matter.

I pulled my phone out from my bag – it was dead. Crawling to where my charger was, I rammed the lead into the phone and waited impatiently for it to come to life. There was only one person I wanted to speak to right now.

Within seconds, my phone lit up and with it came a steady stream of notifications. There were over thirty missed calls from Isaac. I swiped those out of the way and went immediately to my contacts and searched for Jadell. It went straight to voicemail. I checked the time. It was almost 7.30 p.m. on Saturday evening – there was no reason for her to be unreachable unless . . .

I kissed my teeth. She was on a date. She had mentioned that Craig bruddah last night.

I sighed, slumping to the floor.

In theory, there was no confusion:

> Girl's brother is murdered.
>
> Girl leaves home city and moves to God knows where.
>
> Girl ends up going to same school as brother's killer.
>
> Girl likes boy, boy likes girl.
>
> Boy keeps secret from girl.
>
> Girl finds out who he really is.
>
> Girl never speaks to him again.

But in reality, it wasn't so easy.

Was Isaac really the enemy?

A liar, yes.

A killer?

I just couldn't see it.

But had Mike seen the killer in Israel? I doubted it.

You never know who will strike the deadly blow.

Not that any of it mattered any more. No matter how I felt, I knew being with Isaac would never work. My dad was already moving me to a new school.

I swiped at the tears that still flowed freely down my cheeks.

My phone began to vibrate. It was J.

As soon as I answered, all I could hear was yelling.

'And that's how – because you're a fas' likkle hoe that just looks man! There is only one woman in here!' It was Jadell's mum, screaming.

I struggled to sit upright. 'Hello? J, are you there?'

There were noises like someone was running with the phone in their hand. Then I heard a door slam and the sound of a lock clicking. Suddenly there was quiet.

'J?' I asked again, hesitantly.

All I could hear was sniffling and then a sob. I sat up straight. J never cried. 'What's wrong?' I asked, quickly shelving my own problems.

'Cyn . . . I have to tell you something,' she said, and before I could say anything: 'I'm pregnant.'

I felt my stomach drop, the way it does when you're in a lift that's going down.

'Mum is telling me I have to move out whether I keep it or not,' sobbed Jadell. 'She said she's tired of me bringing shame on the family.'

J's mum was a fine one to talk. She had her first baby at fourteen and all five of her kids had different dads. But I knew that cussing her mum wouldn't be helpful now.

'What do you need, babe?' I asked, wanting to help, though I wasn't sure what I could do. The reality was my savings were minimal, I wasn't old enough to drive and I had no idea how to help her decide what to do.

'Do you think I could come and crash at yours? I was going to Craig's tonight but—'

'Hold up, is he the baby's dad?' I asked, worried.

There was a pause.

'I . . . I think so,' she whimpered.

'Oh, J,' I sighed.

'Nah, nah. It will be fine,' she said, trying to firm it.

The beep that indicates an incoming call interrupted her

protest. I didn't have to look at my phone to know who it was. On Jadell's end of the line, I heard someone hammering against a door.

'You'd better be packing your shit in there!' her mum's voice yelled in the background.

'Girl, I gotta go. Wait! How was your date?' she asked suddenly.

'Ummm . . . it was great,' I lied.

'I knew it – I'm so happy for you. Later, gator,' she added hurriedly.

And then the line went dead.

So this is what old folks meant by the saying *when it rains it pours*.

My phone continued to vibrate. I turned it over in my hands as Isaac's name flashed before me. I hit the red button.

A moment later, a series of texts flashed up on the screen.

> I know u don't want to talk to me
> U don't have 2
> But pls let me explain
> I will be in the dog walk fields behind your place tomorrow at midday
> I will wait for one hour

There was a pause, and then a moment later, one more text appeared.

> Please Cyn
>
> x

My stomach flipped, envisioning the absolute carnage that would ensue if I were to take him up on his offer.

I got into bed, but I couldn't sleep. I could hear Mum retelling the story numerous times over the course of the evening. The whole 'what happens in this house stays in this house' only applied once the fourth cousins who lived in Jamaica already knew about your business.

It was close to midnight when Dad slipped in to ask me if I wanted something to eat. He seemed tired.

'Come on, you must keep your strength up,' he gently encouraged.

'For what, Dad?' I asked.

He couldn't find a response, so he left as quietly as he came. Eventually, I must have fallen asleep.

CHAPTER TWENTY-SIX

'You can't blame him.'

I would have recognised that voice anywhere.

I blinked a few times.

There was a young man sitting across from me. Mike? It sure did look like him. And not the last time I saw him, bruised and beaten in a mortuary. This boy was whole, unblemished, handsome even. And, most importantly, alive.

'Cyn? Are you listening to me?' he asked.

I shook my head back and forth. 'Uh yeah, yeah, I'm listening,' I whispered.

'You can't blame him. Like, you don't know the half of it,' he pressed. There was an urgency to his tone that I didn't like. 'You deserve to know the truth.'

'What do you mean?' I asked, anxious. I could sense we didn't have much time.

Mike didn't seem to hear me. 'It wasn't just him. He got caught up,' he said, standing.

I didn't remember him being this tall.

'I don't have much time, little sis,' he finally admitted.

'Don't leave!' I screeched.

'Like I always told you, listen to your intuition,' he said, beginning to walk away.

'Mike! No! Wait!' I screamed, but as I went to reach for him, my hand went straight through his arm.

And then I woke up. It was pitch black in my room, the house quiet.

I sat up, clutching my chest. My breathing was heavy and jagged. I felt damp.

Had that really been Mike? It felt so real. It had to be. But what was the truth he wanted me to know? How many more secrets could there be?

As my breathing calmed, I tried to remember every detail of Mike's face. He'd looked older than he had when he was murdered. Did people continue to age in heaven? *Was* there even a heaven? If there was, how had I gotten there? Had *I* died?

I pinched myself. The immediate pain confirmed that I was very much still alive.

'It was just a dream, Cynthia. Get a grip,' I said to myself.

As I lay in the dark, waiting for dawn, I admitted to myself that I'd suspected for a long time there was more to the story of Mike's death. The revelation that had blown my life apart, now for the second time, was just one branch on a very big tree. And the roots of that tree? Well, that was Mike. Did my brother deserve to die? No, of course not. But what had led to that moment? Why had he become so withdrawn and jumpy? Was it just exam stress . . . or something more sinister? I was both literally and figuratively tired of being in the dark.

I turned on my reading lamp and the golden glow that bathed the room instantly made me feel calmer and safer. Swinging my legs off the side of the bed I reached for my phone and sank to the floor. It was just approaching 3 a.m. Yesterday I'd been too shocked to pore over the letters between Isaac and his brother Israel but now, in the depths of the night, I felt like I had all the time in the world. If Israel hadn't killed Mike, who had? And if it wasn't a mugging gone wrong then what was the real reason?

I scrolled back to Thomas's message and downloaded the images of the letters, saving them to my camera roll. In order to make them easier to read, I decided the best thing to do was airdrop the images to a larger screen. I reached for my laptop.

Once all the files had loaded, I took a deep breath. I reminded myself that nothing could be worse than my current reality. I had already lost two people I loved – even if one was still alive. This was about finally understanding this tragedy once and for all.

The first thing that caught my eye was how beautiful Israel's handwriting was. Every letter wasn't just legible but beautifully formed.

I looked back to the top of the paper, wanting to start at the beginning. HMP Wallbridge. Like Dad had said, there weren't any great universities up there. So Isaac must have only been looking to be closer to Israel. I found this both sweet and deeply saddening. At least he still had a brother to be close to.

Most of the letters contained updates and pleasantries, everyday things. Israel making requests for things like paper, pens and fresh underwear. Isaac updating him about what was happening in his life. There were tender exchanges too, usually about their parents and how much they both wished they were still alive.

Israel consistently reminded Isaac of how lucky he was to be adopted by the Goddards, and he begged Isaac to do right by how blessed he was.

> At the end of the day, I only ended up doing road because there was no other choice for me, bro. You're living the life the elders used to promise us would one day be ours if we just followed their orders. You can't waste it.

I felt wetness on my face and realised I was crying. Although I'd never gotten dragged into that scene, I knew those choices were right there. Look at Auntie June's son. We had all been raised together, played together. And yet Luke had still got caught in the net of violence and crime.

I kept reading and then, a few more letters in, my heart jumped as I spotted something about me.

> Bro, this is mad but the sister of ~~Michael Adeyeke~~ is joining my school.

There was a thick black line blurring out what was undoubtedly Mike's name. It sickened me to see him literally erased. But, more importantly, this meant Isaac had known about me before I even arrived at Thornton's. Oh my God. My mind raced. Maybe this had been a set-up after all, Israel telling Isaac to get close to me, all with the aim of taking revenge . . .

But, to my surprise, in Israel's response, he encouraged Isaac to stay away from me.

Plus it's important to remember that he was no goody-
two-shoes. Only God knows what madness she may be
in. STAY AWAY FROM HER.

'Stay away from me!?' I asked aloud, shocking myself with my
own voice. What a fucking cheek. Me? A whole murderer was
telling his brother to stay away from me? Jesus Christ, I was
now pretty sure that I had died and gone to hell because this
couldn't be happening. I kept reading, even though my anger
was making it hard to concentrate on the words.

There may still be a case on my end, bro. My solicitor
thinks we can try and have this overturned on the
grounds of some work around the joint enterprise law.
Don't make this harder for me, abeg.

I felt my stomach slide towards my toes. Thankfully, I was
sitting down.

Israel was hoping to come out of prison. But how? And,
more pressingly, when? And Isaac had known this all along?

And what was the joint enterprise law?

I hastily opened Google and typed it into the search bar.

I had to click on a few results until I was met with an
explanation I understood:

**Joint Enterprise cases involve crimes where more than
one person takes part. The evidence rules enable those
who did not strike the fatal blow or pull the trigger
nonetheless to be convicted of murder.**

'Rah,' I said aloud to my shadow.

I was no law graduate but for Israel's solicitor to even be talking about it, there had to be some truth to it, didn't there? I hadn't been allowed to go to the trial, so my knowledge of the case was limited. And I'd never had the desire to google anything about it. The way I'd seen it, going searching for things wouldn't give me the one thing I wanted: my brother back. But meeting Isaac, coming perhaps as close as I ever would to sharing the same air as someone who knew what my brother's final moments had been like – it had changed all that. Now I was desperate to know more.

Frenzied, I typed 'Michael Adegoke' and 'trial' into Google and hit search. Immediately, images popped up. Alongside Mike's most recent passport photo there were five other faces, all young men I didn't recognise, except one.

Mum was right, Isaac and Israel looked strikingly similar.

Even though my hands were shaking and I was holding back tears, I kept going.

There had been five of them in total, Mike's attackers.

One had been sixteen. The same age I was now.

Big Mike had been ambushed.

A backpack was taken off him.

He had tried to fight back but there were too many of them.

Four of them had been wielding knives.

'You hacked at Mr Adegoke like a butcher would its merchandise,' the judge was reported as saying.

I quickly closed the window. That was enough.

But then, almost like my body had been possessed, I pushed the laptop off my thighs and stood up slowly. Without giving it too much thought, I inched my way towards my bedroom door and ever so gently turned the handle. I opened the door slowly and held my breath.

Thankfully, Dad was a loud snorer. The sound of his laboured inhales and exhales were loud enough to wake elephants in Africa. I hoped Mum was sleeping too. Where I was going wasn't too far away, but I definitely didn't want to be caught heading there. The bedroom Mum had chosen as Mike's was at the other end of the hall. Trying not to think too much about what I was doing, I tiptoed towards it. By the time I'd turned the handle to Mike's room and slowly inched the door closed behind me, my body was trembling from nerves. I tried to calm my breathing, so I'd hear if anyone was coming. After what felt like an hour, but was likely no more than two minutes, I assessed that the coast was clear.

I turned to face the room. Unlike when I'd come in here previously, I didn't feel haunted or particularly sad this time. I actually felt quite angry.

Mike had been hiding something. I wanted the truth. And if there was any place I could get closer to it, it would be here.

When we moved, Dad and I hadn't had the heart to say that we thought Mum recreating Mike's room in this new space was crazy. But now I was thankful for the sentiments of a grieving mother because it meant I didn't have to go through loads of dusty boxes. Everything had been put out as if, one day, he was going to come home and ask where his socks were. I walked over to his bed and sat on it.

'Diving in and ransacking the place wouldn't be smart, Cyn,' I whispered to myself. I had to think how Mike had thought.

I started with his crystal collection. Some were so precious to him he'd kept them in boxes. Gently, I shook them out, checking underneath each one for something; I wasn't sure what. Every box was empty. I put them back as perfectly as I could.

After the crystals, I turned my attention to his dresser. When we'd moved, Mum hadn't actually packed his clothes, she'd just taped the drawers shut so his smalls wouldn't fall out. I opened the top drawer and one by one I uncurled his socks, which he had stored by rolling one into the other, like each sock was pregnant with another identical sock. Suddenly, I felt something inside one of the pairs. My heart began to race. Quickly, I uncurled them in my hands, realising I had closed my eyes in fear only when I noticed I couldn't see anything. I forced myself to open them, and the shine of whatever it was momentarily blinded me. I brought it closer to the bedroom window, hoping the light of the moon would aid me.

'Uh! Yuck!' I whispered, when I realised it was a packet of condoms. *This guy!* I thought. He had always acted as if he was Mr Virginity himself. Perhaps it had been gyaldem blowing up his phone after all.

I shook my head multiple times, trying to rid my mind of an image no sibling would want to linger on.

I was going to stuff the condoms back in the socks, but then decided against it. If it had been the other way round, I would have wanted him to dispose of anything that could sour the image Mum and Dad had of me. So I shoved the pack into the pocket of my PJ bottoms and made a mental note to dispose of them later. And I put the socks back as precisely as I had found them.

Suddenly, I saw the hallway light go on.

Shit, I thought to myself, panicking. I sank to the floor and pulled my knees into my chest.

Worst-case scenario, if Mum or Dad came in here looking for me, I would just act as if I were feeling the need to be close to Mike after everything that went down.

A few moments later, I heard a toilet flush and then the hallway went dark once more. I maintained my position for another minute, until I was certain the coast was clear, then I stood and looked around the room, deciding where to search next.

Maybe this was a struggle because there was nothing to find. Perhaps I had let the communication between Isaac and Israel plant a rotten seed deep within me, making me distrust Mike for no reason. Maybe *this* was their plan. I mean, all Big Mike ever did was read. His head was always . . .

'IN A BOOK!' I yelped.

Quickly, I threw my hand over my mouth, listening, but there was no noise from down the hall. I let myself relax again. Mike had once told me, 'Cyn, if you ever want to hide something, put it in a book. With everything online now, very few people still have the patience to look to one of the oldest sources of knowledge in the world.'

Well, I had time tonight. I looked up at Mike's bookshelf, full to the brim of encyclopaedias and world-record books. I glanced over at his discoloured Arsenal clock that he'd refused to part with. It was coming up to 4 a.m. A few hours to search for the truth felt like a welcome lifetime after a season of lies.

So I could keep tabs on what books I'd checked, I decided to start from the top and work my way down. I pulled at Mike's old swivel chair that was planted under his desk, needing something to reach the top shelf.

Carefully, I clambered on to it, rising slowly to ensure I was distributing my weight correctly. Once I felt as safe as one could when snooping in their dead brother's room in the middle of the night while balancing unsteadily on a wobbly office chair, I began to pull out the books on the top shelf one by one, flicking through their pages. The first few were normal books. But when I picked up the seventh, I could immediately tell that something was different. All seven were part of the same encyclopaedic set, but this one didn't match the weight of the others. That made alarm bells ring.

Holding the book to my chest, I carefully stepped down from the chair. I turned the book over in my shaking hands, already feeling as though I wanted to cry. Perching on the edge of Mike's bed, I opened it up. The book was hollow. Where there should have been pages of words, there was instead a deep cavity, where the paper had been removed. Inside was a tiny black notebook, the sort that might come in a Christmas cracker. I lifted it out and held it between my forefinger and thumb. Opening it cautiously, I saw it contained lists of numbers. They looked like mobile numbers, but they had no names next to them.

I jammed the tiny notebook into my bra, then turned my attention towards the other item in the book, a larger package, wrapped up in Christmas paper. It was rectangular and not very

253

heavy. I shook it gently, hoping for a clue as to its contents, worried that whatever it was would change my thoughts about Mike for ever, but it made no sound. I stuffed it into the waistband of my knickers, doing a little jig to ensure that the package wouldn't fall as I walked back to my room.

I pushed the swivel chair back to the desk with the purposefulness of someone who knew that the hunt was over. After pausing to make sure the house was still asleep, I slipped out of my brother's room, closing the door as quietly as I could, and half jogged down the hall.

I didn't breathe until I was back in my room. My bedroom door didn't have a lock. But my bathroom did. I snatched my phone off the floor and went into my bathroom, quickly locking the door behind me. I whipped the package out of my waistband and threw it into the sink, where it landed with a gentle thud. Turning my back on it, I marched up and down in the small space, trying to talk myself out of what I knew I was going to do regardless.

I rummaged around in my bra for the tiny notebook, then sat on the toilet and began to type the first number into my phone.

Just as I was about to hit the green button, I realised I hadn't blocked my own number.

I deleted it and began again, this time starting with the digits that would make sure I came up on the other person's line as 'No Caller ID'.

I took one last breath and hit call.

Immediately, I was met with a high-pitched sound and then a voice that said, 'It seems you have dialled an incorrect number. Please check the number and try again.'

I hung up, using the back of my hand to mop the beads of sweat now forming on my brow. But I still wasn't discouraged.

I dialled the second number.

This time, my ears were hit with three high-pitched beeps and nothing else.

I was so sure the third number wouldn't work, that when it began to ring, I almost dropped the phone. I quickly reached for my flannel and jammed it into my mouth, worried that whoever might answer would know who I was just from the sound of my breathing.

One the third ring, someone picked up.

I stopped breathing altogether, waiting for them to say hello. But they never did. They just waited, listening, seeing if I would make the first sound.

After a stand-off that felt like an eternity, they finally spoke.

'I hope whoever is using a dead motherfucker's phone knows that *they'll* be dead soon if I don't get my shit back.' The voice was deep and so sinister it sent chills down my spine.

I scrambled to hang up, dropping the phone in my haste and fear. When I picked it up, I saw there was an almighty crack on the screen. I wondered if that's how my heart now looked too. I tried to steady my breathing, but I was scared.

For the first time since deciding to play detective, I considered telling Mum and Dad.

No, they've been through enough, I thought.

'The police?' I asked aloud.

I shook my head.

Whoever had been on the other end of the phone clearly

wasn't scared of the police. Getting the cops involved could just put me in danger.

Considering what was happening to her, I deffo couldn't bring this to Jadell.

I had never felt more alone.

I suddenly remembered the Christmas present in the sink.

I looked over my shoulder at it.

Gingerly, I leaned over the sink and prodded the package masquerading as an innocent present. With nothing else left to try, I decided to go for it, and like a toddler on Christmas morning, I tore at the paper.

When the contents were revealed, I was so stunned that I dropped the whole thing. I stood there, body frozen, as my brain moved at one thousand miles an hour.

Was *this* what the guy on the phone wanted back? If this had been mine and someone had taken it, then I sure as hell would be angry too.

I couldn't be sure how much it was, but I guessed at least ten thousand pounds, all in fifty-pound notes.

Where the hell had Mike got that kind of cash from?

I sank to my knees, using my arms as a pillow on the edge of the toilet lid.

'Mike . . . who were you really?' I asked aloud.

I sat there as my brain continued to piece the puzzle together.

Is this why his phone was always blowing up?

Is this why he had become withdrawn and snappy?

Is this why he hadn't wanted Dad to drop him off at campus that day?

'Mike, no!' I hissed, suddenly overwhelmed by the betrayal.

I could hear birds tweeting in agreement. I checked the time on my cracked phone screen. It was almost 5 a.m. Dad would be getting up soon. I had to think fast.

Where could I hide this stuff until I made up my mind how best to handle it?

My bedroom wasn't safe, considering how Mum went through her surprise cleaning moments.

A wardrobe felt too bait.

And somewhere away from the house was out of the question.

For some reason I didn't want to put it back where I'd found it, in Big Mike's room.

How about right here? a voice said in my head, as my eyes were drawn to the bath. I knocked softly on the side panel and was rewarded by a hollow sound. I softly pushed at the panel, hoping for some movement. Thankfully, it seemed to be just slotted in, rather than glued in any way, and with each poke I was able to nudge it out a bit more, until I had created a space wide enough for my hand to fit through.

'Yes,' I whispered, rising to my feet and collecting the cash, the wrapping paper and the tiny notebook from the sink. I hastily returned to the bath and stuffed the contents of Mike's book into the space I'd revealed. Once I'd knocked the panel back into place, I took that as my cue to collapse. So I did, crying on the bathroom floor until the sun came up.

CHAPTER TWENTY-SEVEN

By the time I heard Dad get up, I was still curled on my bathroom floor. I had a banging headache and my thoughts had been racing for hours.

Where had the money come from? A lifetime of saved pocket money? No, the money hidden underneath the bath was more money than I'd seen in my entire life, and our pocket money hadn't exactly come in fifty-pound notes. A job at uni? No, Mike hadn't even worked part-time because Dad wanted him to focus solely on his studies. My mind was racing towards the only possible conclusion, but I didn't want to accept it.

There was only one walk of life that I knew of which could provide you with that level of cash and it broke my heart to now know that Big Mike was somehow connected to it.

I couldn't shake the memory of that sinister voice either. Once my panic had receded, I'd turned that call over and over in my mind. I now realised I'd dialled a burner phone that only Mike had the number of. And Mr Sinister wanted his money back.

The buzz of my own phone snapped me back to reality. Nervously, I glanced at the text. Even though I knew I had blocked my number before calling the burner phone, what if *that* voice had a way of tracing me? I breathed a sigh of relief to see it was only a text from Isaac.

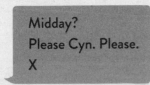

Midday?
Please Cyn. Please.
X

I let out a long sigh. As much as I didn't want to meet with Isaac, in some ways I felt I had no choice. Even though he had been lying to me, so had Mike. Not that I would ever tell Isaac that. Or anyone for that matter. I'd already decided that I would rather die before I became a snitch. Talking of snitches, I thought of Thomas. I hated him even more for doing this now. In his messages he had tried to say that this was about me, about making sure I knew the truth, but I knew that it was really about spite. Boys like him, privileged boys who always got their own way, grew up to be privileged men who would stop at – and be stopped by – nothing. I scrolled to his name and blocked his number.

At around 11.30 a.m. I heard the front door go and then Mum's car driving off. Mum leaving made my escape plan a little easier. I knew Dad would likely be locked in his study, figuring out the logistics of getting me into a new school by Monday.

I didn't debate my outfit. I was beyond trying to impress Isaac. I threw on a grey tracksuit, a black puffer vest and some battered kicks. I hadn't been to those fields where Isaac wanted to meet, but I knew the pathway that would take me there because it was signposted at the bottom of our road.

Just as I was leaving my room, I remembered the condoms I'd hidden in my PJs. Hastily I retrieved them and stuffed them into the inside pocket of my puffer vest. Thank God I hadn't forgotten about them. It didn't bear thinking about what would go down if Dad had found them while loading the washing machine.

I came down the stairs as quietly as possible, tiptoeing past my dad's closed office door, through which I could hear him talking on the phone. I left a note on the kitchen table saying I was going for a walk for some fresh air, just in case he came out or Mum came back before I returned and stepped outside. It was chilly. The days were getting shorter and colder, and the soft crunch of frost-bitten grass beneath my feet confirmed that winter was coming.

I checked my phone. It was now 12.15 p.m. I hadn't responded to Isaac's message. I just trusted that he would be there.

The air was crisp and even though my note about needing fresh air had been a lie, somehow, I did feel like I could breathe better out here, be *more mindful* as Mrs Crabtree would have put it. I waited until I was a little away from the house and then retrieved the condoms from my pocket. I took a sharp look around before lobbing the packet into some nearby bushes and then walked on as if nothing had happened.

'You owe me one, Mike,' I whispered angrily.

If only getting rid of the money and the little black book were that easy, I thought to myself.

As I got closer to the meeting spot, I began to feel short of breath, the panic creeping up into my chest. I tried one of the mindfulness techniques Mrs Crabtree had taught us, where you counted to ten, paused, and then started again, repeating until you felt calm. I did this three times, focusing on the sound of my feet on the grass, and the panic subsided a bit. A few dog walkers went past and then some kids on bikes, but I didn't pay them much attention. I kept my focus on the counting until I spotted a stationary figure up ahead. As I neared, I could see it was Isaac. Next to him on the ground was a large black bike. He'd cycled here.

My heart started to race again. Part of me wanted to run back home. Only now did it occur to me how dangerous this was. What if this was a set-up? I used to hear about it a lot at St Martin's, girls being used to lure boys into a deadly situation. Was this the reverse of that? Was I thinking with my heart and not my head?

All these questions and yet I kept walking forward. It was as if I were tethered to an invisible piece of string that someone else was in control of.

'I'm so sorry, Cyn,' he said as soon as I was in earshot.

Despite everything that had happened, the sound of his voice still sent my stomach fluttering.

'Me too,' I sighed, stopping in front of him. 'But that's not enough to fix what's happened,' I went on, standing up straight.

He recoiled as if my words were a punch in the gut.

'I made a mistake,' he said firmly, stepping towards me. 'I should have told you the truth about who I was. But I'm not my brother. And I'm not a bad person. You know that, Cyn. If not, you wouldn't have come to meet me.'

Up close, I could see that his usually fresh face was zapped of all its energy. He looked as tired and scared as I felt. Again, as if I were a puppet bending to someone else's will, I found myself taking another step towards him.

'Can you forgive me?' Isaac asked. 'I know I fucked up, but . . . I love you.'

'No, you don't,' I sighed.

'Listen, I don't know what else to call it cos I've never felt this way for someone before. You're on my mind when I wake up and when I go to sleep, when I'm doing coursework, when I'm eating, when I'm brushing my teeth. You're as constant as my breath.'

I blinked a few times, hoping it would help my tears stay back.

I almost smiled. 'It's not that easy.'

'I know,' he admitted. 'But it's not impossible, is it? That's what love is; it's about feeling this way even when you're not supposed to.'

This time I did smile, but it was a sad one. 'It *is* impossible,' I said. 'Maybe I could forgive you lying to me, one day, but my family will never forgive who your brother is.'

Isaac became visibly rigid. 'Cyn, there's more to the story . . .' he began, kicking the tyre on his bike.

'I keep hearing that! Well, since I'm the main fucking character, how about you finish it?' I yelled, throwing my hands in the air, my temper finally getting the better of me.

'Cyn, Mike was pushing, you know?' Isaac whispered, his voice so low I could have pretended to have misheard what he said.

'Pushing what? A bike?' I asked, trying to laugh. Even though

Isaac was confirming what I'd already guessed, I wasn't ready to accept it. Not yet.

Isaac just shifted his weight from foot to foot, like he had ants in his socks. My defensiveness was rising, but so was the memory of the money and the little black book now hiding behind my bath panel. I shook the image away.

'The way Israel tells the story is that they went there that night to collect some weight from your brother . . . and when they went to exchange, Mike switched up the price. Then all hell broke loose.' He sighed, not looking at me but past me, into the distance.

I felt light-headed and blindly stretched out my hand, hoping to find something that I could use to steady myself. Isaac reached out and I felt myself fall against him. The field was spinning.

'Israel just got caught up,' I whispered, remembering what dream-Mike had said. I wanted to keep defending my brother. That's what a sibling was supposed to do. But even my acting had limits.

'What did you say?' Israel asked, still supporting me.

'Nothing,' I said, closing down, the panic rising in my chest once more. I began counting again, and when I reached ten, I took a step backwards, out of Isaac's supportive hold. I immediately felt colder. In just a few short weeks, Isaac had become my constant. He was the silver lining in this rain-filled cloud that just wouldn't leave me alone. I loved him. I didn't want to imagine my life without him. But I didn't have a choice.

My phone began to ring. It was Mum.

I made a quiet sign at Isaac and answered.

'Hi, Mum!' I said a little too cheerfully.

'Cyn . . . listen, Jadell's here. We need you to come home.' She spoke as if she were trying to hold back tears.

'I'm coming right now,' I responded, before cutting the call.

'Is everything OK?' Isaac asked, looking worried.

'You know what, considering how my life is going I highly doubt it.' I laughed mirthlessly. 'Goodbye, Isaac,' I said, turning to walk away from him.

'Cyn, wait! What about us?' he pleaded, sounding panicked.

I turned back to face him. 'There is no "us" any more, Isaac. Don't you get it? Because of what happened between our brothers this will never, ever work, for either of us. There is always going to be fear and resentment and anger.'

He opened his mouth to protest, but I cut him off.

'Falling in love with you . . . it was the easiest thing in the world. Because you know where I'm from, what I've been through. You understand me better than anyone,' I said, the words coming fast and hard now. 'But don't you see? That was our downfall too. Our worlds are too close, too intertwined. It cuts both ways. There are no winners here,' I finished, turning from him again and continuing to make my way across the field.

'You can't just ignore me for ever! We're in the same class, Cyn. Come on,' he said, jogging behind me to catch up.

Something in me wanted to see his heart break, to shatter into a billion unfixable pieces so he could feel the way I did. I turned back towards him, knowing this was the last time we would be together. The cost of loving him was too high. My family had already paid the ultimate price.

'Dad has pulled me out. I start a new school next week.' I watched as his face fell, but it didn't make me feel any better. I turned towards home again, following the same path that had brought me here.

'Everything I love, I lose,' I heard him say.

'Same,' I whispered.

And then I started to run, so fast that my tears went sideways instead of down. I wasn't just running away from him, but from the heartache, the heaviness and, most painful of all, the truth. I didn't want to be the one who tarnished the perfect image we all had of Mike, so I just kept on running and running, until I knew Isaac couldn't see me, and I couldn't see him, until I imagined that I could run right out of all of this and start all over again.

EPILOGUE

The sound of CJ crying tore through my nightmare.

It was the usual one – Mr Sinister coming at me wielding a machete. Yet again, I'd woken just as he caught the back of my jacket.

Man, for a three-month-old, that baby had a proper set of lungs. But before I could even swing myself out of bed, he'd stopped crying and I knew that Mum already had him in her arms. It made me wonder why she chastised me and J for picking him up so much.

'You lot are going to spoil that boy; you're giving him too much hand,' she would say, before taking CJ from us and doing exactly what she'd just told us not to do.

A year ago, after the last time I'd seen Isaac, I had run all the way home to find J in our living room. Her mum had turned her out and Craig wasn't returning her calls. She literally had nowhere else to go. Dad and I had both stood there in shock when Mum suggested that she could make room for J in what would have been Mike's room.

'You fucking what?!' J had squealed that first evening, after I'd told her who Isaac really was.

'Shhhh,' I begged. 'Listen, I don't even want to bring him up around Mum and Dad right now, so keep it down.'

'Bloody hell, Cyn. Wa gagwarn really? I'm pregnant and homeless, and you're in love with the brother of your brother's murderer. We actually deserve a reality show.' She sighed, flopping on the edge of Mike's bed next to me.

I went to giggle but instead burst into tears.

'No, no, no, babe, don't cry. Not after some woteless yoot,' she begged, quickly getting up to close the bedroom door.

'You. Don't. Understand,' I sobbed. 'I really loved him.' Even though it was true, I regretted it the moment I said it. Now – when she couldn't even get a text back from the father of her child – wasn't the time to remind her that she perhaps hadn't yet been loved at all.

If she did feel a way, she didn't miss a beat.

'Oh, Cyn. There are more guys, man. This is just . . . really not it. Someone who lies to you from the beginning isn't the love of your life,' she said, sounding more grown up than I'd ever heard before.

So I sucked up my tears and decided to focus on her and the baby, essentially my little niece or nephew. And what was supposed to be a few nights had turned into J moving in permanently and me helping her study for her exams while she grew a whole new human. Dad hadn't been sure at first but watching how Mum came alive because she had someone else to take care of eventually trumped all of his worries. And having J around was a welcome distraction from all that had happened to me too. I had desperately wanted to share *everything* I knew with her, but I loved her too much to put her at risk. So I'd kept it to the bare minimum.

After my experience at Thornton's I didn't even try to make

friends once I started at Denbey's. I just kept my head down and focused on my work. Even with the disruption of moving yet again, I came out with GCSE results high enough to stay on there for sixth form too.

J living with us helped time fly and soon there was a kid around, who I hoped would one day call me auntie. The plan now was that J and CJ would stay with us until the council were able to offer her a place.

'Do you miss him?' J asked out of the blue one day a few weeks after CJ was born, while I was helping fold away some baby clothes Mum had washed.

'Every day,' I said. There was still only one 'him'. As much as I still stood by the only decision I could have made, that didn't erase my heartache. I'd done everything I could to move on – blocking him on social media, deleting his texts, donating all the clothes that reminded me of him – but I couldn't stop myself from dreaming about him. I wasn't sure whether it was the nightmare of the faceless man with the machete or the dreams where Isaac and I were together and happy that made me wake up feeling worse.

And then there was still the issue of the things that belonged to Big Mike. At the start, I would check the bath space multiple times a day, half hoping that one day I would squeeze my elbow through that little gap and everything would be gone, and with it the responsibility of whatever loose ends there were to tie up. But sure enough, every time there it was, a constant reminder of Mike's betrayal. As time went on, I checked the spot less frequently, sometimes going days without even acknowledging its existence at all.

Then finally, a day came when I could ignore it no longer.

The tub in my bathroom was smaller than the others in the house and sometimes J would bathe little CJ in there as it was easier for us to get him in and out.

On this particular day, we got distracted after we started running the water, and by the time J and I had returned to the bathroom with the baby we had all but flooded the place.

'Shit,' she panicked. 'Your folks have been too good to me for me to come and mash up their place literally weeks before CJ and I get offered a place of our own. Bring more towels! Quickly!' she barked. I hastily put CJ down safely in his cot in J's room and then ran to the airing cupboard, where I had to get a stepladder to reach the old towels.

'Rah, it's gone everywhere, man! Even under the bath, I think,' I heard her moan.

It took only a few seconds for me to register what she would do next. When I did, I came off the ladder so fast that a pile of towels came tumbling down on me. I stumbled to my feet and raced back to my bathroom, trying to prevent the inevitable, but by the time I arrived in the doorway J was standing in a huge puddle of water, with the money in one hand and the tiny book in the other, both now drenched.

'Babe, you got something you wanna tell me?' she whispered, her eyes as wide as saucers.

I let out a long sigh. 'Now listen, this has to stay between you and me.'

And so I began the story.

AUTHOR'S NOTE

When I was very young, knife crime in the UK – especially in the Black community – was a big focus, and synonymous with one name. Stephen Lawrence. As I got older, the fear of knife crime was blanketed by gun crime. With firearms being such a concern, in 1998, Operation Trident, a community-led initiative to tackle gun crime, was announced. But as with most things in life, when we make one thing our primary focus, it allows other issues to go unchecked.

For many reasons, young people today are being drawn towards the blade again, and knife crime is now back on the map.

Children dying due to wounds from a knife attack now happens so frequently that, unless you're looking, you may no longer even see an image of the recently deceased. Bright flames are being blown out so quickly, even the internet is struggling to keep up. To make it easier, the headlines now just seem to include the age, gender and location.

Not even a name.

I would need more space than I have here to list the names of all the young lives lost since that fateful night Stephen Lawrence was killed in 1993. But it is important to remember that no matter how briefly it is reported, every one of these deaths is a young person whose life -- for no good reason - was cut short. There is no one 'typo' of person more likely to be a victim than someone else. We are living in times when, as the kids say, 'anyone can get it'.

So, if you're a young person who has particular worries in regards to knife crime, please, please speak to either your parents, guardians or teachers, or take advantage of some of the resources included at the end of this book.

If you're a parent who has read this book, please continue to engage with your child/children about knife crime, its harsh realities and consequences.

And for now, please take some time to remember the children who are no longer with us.

JOINT ENTERPRISE

The concept of 'joint enterprise' that led to Isaac's brother Israel being imprisoned for Big Mike's murder in this story is actually a real law in the UK.

Joint enterprise allows multiple defendants to all be convicted of the same crime, even if they were involved in different ways or to different extents. It means that someone who assisted or encouraged someone else to commit a crime could be convicted for the crime itself.

The law has been heavily criticised. A study by the Institute of Criminology at the University of Cambridge revealed that this law is used disproportionately against young Black boys and men. In 2016 the Supreme Court ruled that it had been misinterpreted and misused for the last thirty years and limited its reach.

As of the time this book went to print, however, it is still being used.

SOURCE:

https://www.thebureauinvestigates.com/stories/2014-09-02/joint-enterprise-disproportionately-affects-black-men-according-to-institute-of-criminology

SUPPORT

If you need support or want more information on the issues raised in this book, here are some organisations that may be able to help:

ABIANDA
A London-based social enterprise working with young women affected by gangs and county lines.
abianda.com

THE BEN KINSELLA TRUST
One of the leading anti-knife crime charities in the UK, set up following the tragic murder of Ben Kinsella in 2008.
benkinsella.org.uk

BLUEPRINT FOR ALL
Formerly the Stephen Lawrence Charitable Trust, they work with young people, communities and organisations to create an inclusive society in which everyone, regardless of race, ethnicity or background is provided with tangible opportunities to thrive.
blueprintforall.org

FAMILIES OUTSIDE
Support families in Scotland affected by imprisonment.
familiesoutside.org.uk

FEARLESS
Fearless is a service that allows individuals to pass on information about crime 100% anonymously.
fearless.org/en

HOWARD LEAGUE FOR PENAL REFORM
Working for less crime, safer communities and fewer people in prison. Run a confidential legal service for young people under 21, including those in prison.
Call free 0808 801 0308 / 0808 802 0153
howardleague.org

JUST FOR KIDS LAW
Work with and for young people to ensure their legal rights are respected and promoted, and their voices heard and valued.
justforkidslaw.org

LIVES NOT KNIVES
A youth-led charity that works to prevent knife crime, serious youth violence and school exclusions by engaging, educating and empowering.
livesnotknives.org

PRISON ADVICE AND CARE TRUST (PACT)

Provides support for prisoners, people with convictions and their families.

prisonadvice.org.uk

POWER THE FIGHT

A charity that tackles violence affecting young people by creating long-term solutions for sustainable change.

powerthefight.org.uk

safe4me

Provides educators, service providers and parents with information and resources to help educate, guide and support children and young people to keep safe.

safe4me.co.uk

STEEL WARRIORS

An anti-knife crime charity that melts down knives taken off the streets and recycles the steel into outdoor street gyms.

steelwarriors.co.uk

ACKNOWLEDGEMENTS

The highest level of thanks to The Goddess – always.

My darling love Bodé – Without you, in so many ways, this version of this story would still be unfertilised. Those few glasses of wine have led to the love story of a generation, and I am very grateful for your ear, encouragement and insight. Thank you.

Esmé-Olivia & RJ – Thank you both for always allowing mummy to retain creative space. Both your lives are a constant stream of inspiration for me. Thank you for allowing me to quench my thirst.

To Gillie Russell – Huge thanks for holding my hand and guiding me through this process. Here is to many more.

Lena McCauley – Thank you for giving me space to work in the best way for me but also gently showing me where I could stretch myself. A book is only as good as its editor and you're brilliant.

Katy Follain – I must thank you for giving me the space in my adult writing schedule to be able to give birth to this.

FZ! Francesca Zampi! My true ride or die. Do you remember before book one you made me get rid of that agent and I was unsure? Yeah, thanks for that. Let's raise a glass of B&B to the future empire.

KJ! Katie-Jane Sullivan – Thank you for keeping it all together when I just want to fall apart.

Leeanne Adu – Thank you for not only helping shape our business but also finding time in the calendar so books like this even get to fruition.

To everyone at The Found – Thank you for always being down to jump in unfamiliar waters.

Remi – Thank you for being ten toes – always.

Leona – Thank you for your prayers and guidance.

Emma – Thank you for always supporting and defending me.

To the Candie Canes! My day ones! Those of you who have been here forever and a day, I cannot fathom how this would not only be possible but also enjoyable without the love and support you all give me. Thank you so much.

And lastly, to any new readers this book may have found, thank you for stepping into the world I created.

Cx

Want to be the first to hear about the best new teen and YA reads?

Want exclusive content, offers and competitions?

Want to chat about books with people who love them as much as you do?

Look no further...

bkmrk

Find your place

@teambkmrk

SNEAK PEAKS

BONUS CONTENT

OFFERS AND GIVEAWAYS

See you there!

bkmrk.co.uk

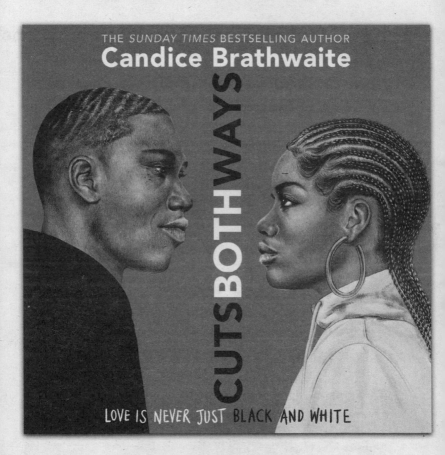